Dog Jack

by Florence W. Biros

Sonrise Publications
New Wilmington, Pennsylvania

Cover Illustration by
R. DiCianni
Models for the cover were Carl Mack & Snowflake

Library of Congress 88-92358
ISBN 0-936369-47-7

Publications & Distribution
Rt. 3, Box 202 • New Wilmington, PA 16142
(412) 946-8334

Many people added their input, enthusiasm and support to the task of bringing *Dog Jack* into print. Special gratitude goes to my husband, Jim; Melva Libb who spent long hours editing and adding finishing touches; Rosine Bucher, historian; the staff at the Soldiers and Sailors Memorial Hall; Marc A. Carr; Bill Hand, Jr.; David Croyle who took the pictures included in the book; and Ravenel Scott and the staff of Faith Printing Company of Taylors , S.C. Special thanks goes to the Gettysburg National Memorial Park and the men who participated in the 1988 reenactment, along with the willing helpers at Buhl Henderson Library at Sharon, PA., and to Joyce Hart. My heartfelt gratitude goes to John Wishner and Edward T. McDougal for their acts of encouragement along with Sarah Nichols Brown and Warren Brown.

TRIBUTE TO A SOLDIER

In an obscure corner of the Allegheny County Soldiers and Sailors Memorial Hall in Pittsburgh, Pennsylvania, there is a faded snapshot of a dog, along with a tribute to the canine soldier who followed his friends into battle and fought side by side with them. The tribute written beneath the snapshot and the feelings written about the dog recorded by Chaplain A.M. Stewart in his book, *Camp, March and Battlefield*, supplied the major details which have been the basis of this Civil War story.

Of necessity, most of the characters and events have been fictionalized, but the story of one of America's little-known war heroes, DOG JACK, in essence is true....

Soldiers' and Sailors' Memorial Hall.

FOREWORD

"THE WORLD WILL LITTLE NOTE NOR LONG REMEMBER WHAT WE SAY HERE."

These words were a part of Honest Abe Lincoln's Gettysburg address. How was he to know he was speaking an untruth – that his speech would be memorized by students for generations to come? When some friends and I walked on the battlefield at Gettysburg one hundred and twenty-five years later, the words of the slave emancipator flashed through my mind.

The stage was set for the reenactment of the bloodiest battle in our nation's history. Stone fences were the same; sentries on guard duty walked the perimeter with their rifles slung across their shoulders. Soldiers in blue perched on canvas stools in front of pup tents. On that humid July day in 1988, a soldier raised his canteen to his lips, just as one would have done a century and a quarter before. Our visit had whisked us back to another era – the most devastating time in our nation's history, when father fought son, brother fought brother. The North fought the South, with the Union nearly becoming split into two segments permanently.

On Gettysburg's rolling Pennsylvania terrain the "enemy" was also present. Soldiers in gray, the Confederates, were stationed on the other side of the stone fences. Some rode

CAVALRY CHARGE...a 9x5 foot painting by Thor Thulstrup

on the backs of shimmering mares and stallions.

Out of the woods marched one of the Union's fife and drum corps. My own heart raced a little faster to the beat of the drummer boy. The significance of what had taken place on those same grounds became even more real as we read the inscriptions on marble and granite markers telling where thousands and thousands of men had died in bloody hand-to-hand combat.

We watched as battles were staged, as cannons roared and bayonets clashed. Men on horseback charged each other. We witnessed the simulated amputation of a Confederate soldier's leg in a barn standing on the foundation of the original edifice which had been so riddled with bullets that it had to be replaced. Realizing that the severing of the young man's limb was staged somehow didn't change the awesome feeling of knowing many Americans lost their limbs, their lives in a building which stood on the same spot.

Our trip to Gettysburg to relive history came because of my interest in a dog — one who'd raced across similar battlefields with the men of the 102nd Pennsylvania Regiment and tended to the wounded. His involvement in the war is wrapped up in the story told here.

The dog had been my initial reason for writing this book. I'd found his pictures in the archives of the Soldiers and Sailors Memorial Hall in Pittsburgh and had initially wanted to know more about his involvement in the war, because he looked like such a mongrel. Yet as I learned more about him, I became intrigued with the facts of the war and the faith of the chaplain who ministered to the regiment and befriended Dog Jack. Jed, the slave boy, Matt, the fireman and many of the circumstances are fictionalized. However, the war, the dog and the chaplain are authentic, as are as many of the facts as possible.

Through this book allow me to take you into our roots with the realization that "We hold these truths to be self-evident — that all men are created equal." Yet today the battle for freedom, justice and equality continues to rage. Vigilance should still be our watchword, if we hope to maintain what our forefathers fought to achieve for us.

Florence W. Biros

Contents

Chapter 1
The Intruder

Jed had put off most of his chores as stable boy at the Pittsburgh Firehouse until early evening because that July day in 1861 had been so humid. While pitching hay up into the loft the sudden feeling hit him that someone or something was standing behind him. Ever since his escape from slavery, he'd had recurring nightmares about his past, and any unexpected movement still caused him to panic.

Whirling about, his eyes focused on the wobbliest, most woe-begone creature he'd ever seen. Jed thought the dog looked ridiculous as it stood warily watching him with one of its eyes comically circled by a brown and black patch, its ribs protruding from beneath its white coat. Jed's heart went out to the animal. He knew all too well what it felt like to be a frightened, tired stray.

Leaning for a moment on his pitchfork, Jed held out his hand. "Here, boy, here," but the apprehensive dog bared its teeth and snarled. What was he going to do to gain its confidence? For a moment he contemplated, then ran to the left corner of the stable where he kept his own meager belongings. Digging deep into his hay mattress, Jed's fingers grasped a small tin box which he removed from its hiding place. He flipped open the lid, then counted the pieces of candy inside — five peppermints he'd been hoarding for three months. Candy was an extra delight to him, for while he was a slave boy in Virginia he'd never had the joy of tasting any. The men at the fire station had given it to him as a present on an April day which he'd always assumed was his fourteenth birthday. He'd kept the candy hidden and had eaten pieces only on days that were special to him.

Upon picking up one of his precious tidbits, sticky from the humidity, he toyed with it in his black fingers, pondering for a moment whether or not he should part with any of it. But one glance at his neglected-looking visitor convinced him that he should. Placing one piece in the palm of his hand, he held it out. "Here, here, fellow. I know what it's like to have an empty stomach. Ya can't be a slave boy pickin' 'backer for years without knowin' what misery is!"

Cautiously the dog sniffed at the candy, then startled Jed by grabbing it suddenly with his mouth. Snap! With one gulp it was gone! Jed was taken back momentarily – why had he given some of his treasure to this dog? He hadn't even taken time to taste it!

But then the dog's tri-colored tail wagged. Jed grinned. Knowing the dog had appreciated his sacrificial gift of hospitality, Jed reached for one more piece of peppermint – far more willing to part with it now that he saw the animal was warming up to him. Two more pieces convinced the dog to let the stable boy stroke his short, bristled fur. Jed gave a smile of smug satisfaction. He'd found himself a new friend!

For several days he tried to keep the animal's presence a secret by tying him out of sight behind the harness rack in the stable. Finally some of the firemen noticed him, but no one informed Jed that the dog would have to leave. Feeling somewhat secure because of their indifference, Jed relaxed and worked hard to get the dog's complete trust.

The decision about whether the dog would be totally accepted and allowed to stay remained with one man – Matt, the fire chief, who'd been out of town visiting his ailing father for nearly two weeks. Realizing Matt, worried about his sick parent, would probably be easily upset, Jed was greatly concerned about how the chief would react to the new tenant in the stable.

The day Matt came back to his duties, a first-thing-in-the-morning fire call came through, so Jed had no choice but to wait for his return to learn of his response to the dog's presence.

It didn't take long for Jed to find out. At the sudden sound of approaching wagon wheels, the cords in the back of Jed's neck became instantly taut. The long, low, horse-drawn fire engine clattered down Pittsburgh's Penn Avenue toward the Niagara Volunteer Fire Engine House. Running to open the firehouse doors, Jed arrived at the entrance the same time the wagon turned into the driveway. "Ho!" Matt ordered from atop his perch on the driver's seat. His command brought the perspiring steeds to an abrupt halt.

"Put the horses back in the stable, Jed, boy," Matt ordered. "You'd best give them a rubdown, too. They've had quite a work out."

Jed looked up at the man who'd become his boss. No matter how often he stood beside him, he never ceased to be amazed at Matt's large body. His great hands, his wide shoulders, his tremendous height were awesome to Jed whose young, lean body would fit comfortably under Matt's arm.

"Yes, suh, Mistah Matt," Jed replied, moving to unharness the team that faithfully pulled the red fire wagon. Busy with the task of unharnessing the doubletrees, Jed momentarily forgot the dog until he heard Matt's voice growl angrily from behind him, "Get out of here, you mangy mutt!"

Jed turned just in time to see the toe of Matt's massive fireman's boot connect with the back hind leg of the stray. With one tremendous yowl the dog went sailing through the air and landed on the fire station floor with such a thud that Jed felt his own heart had landed with it. The dog began to moan and Jed's eyes grew wide with alarm. How could Matt kick such a poor, friendless animal in such a way?

"Mistah Matt!" Jed cried. "What ya go and kick that lost dog fo'?"

"I didn't mean to kick him so hard," Matt grumbled, "but he knows how I feel now! We don't need no dogs around here!"

Seconds later tall, slender George Brown arrived on the scene. "What's going on?" this brown-haired, blue-eyed fireman demanded as he stared at the motionless dog on the floor. It made no sound except an occasional whine which tore at Jed's heart. The fear in the animal's glaring eyes moved Jed. He'd had times when he'd been wounded by vicious and unjustified blows and had been unable to resist his attacker.

"What's the matter with that dog?" George demanded.

"I gave him a boot!" Matt declared emphatically, then added in a less-certain tone of voice, "Musta kicked the mutt harder than I thought...."

George frowned, then walked over beside the dog and leaned down. "Easy, boy, easy. I won't hurt you," he spoke soothingly. "Just want to see where your trouble is."

Matt, too, ambled over to examine the extent of the dog's injury. Jed's stomach began to churn uneasily about what Matt might do next, yet he felt fairly certain that by this time he knew Matt well enough to realize his big friend was having second thoughts about what he had done. Matt always acted impulsively, then was sorry later. His mood could change from wrath to delight, furor to glee in a matter of seconds.

After George examined the dog's hind leg, he declared, "Looks broken to me. See how the back leg bone juts out!"

Matt's face tinged pink, then crimson, "Aw, it couldn't be," he protested. "I didn't kick him THAT hard!"

George's eyes fell to Matt's boot and he shook his head. "I don't know," he teased, "but I'd sure hate to have you use one of those size thirteens on me!"

Even with Jed's great concern for the dog, he couldn't help but grin at George's remark. George and the other firemen often tormented Matt about his big feet.

One glance at Matt's face told Jed that his friend was not amused. "All right, wise guy, you've had your little joke,"

Matt snorted. "Now, what are we going to do with this stupid-looking animal?"

Jed knew Matt's description was right. Admittedly, this dog was one of the homeliest he'd ever seen. "Looks like he's part bull dog, Mistah Matt," Jed suggested.

"Bull dog, ha!" Matt retorted. "This dog's got more mixed-up ancestry than an African Chinese!" Matt started to howl with delight at his clever comparison until his eyes met Jed's. He sensed immediately he had hit upon a sore spot, remembering Jed hated for anyone to make joking references to another person's race.

Jed chose to say nothing about the matter, but declared instead: "Cain't ya help 'im, Mistah Matt? Breakin' mah heart lettin' that poor dog jes' lay there."

"Reckon you're right, boy," he answered, then turned to George who continued to soothe the dog with slow gentle pats. "What do you think we really ought to do — shoot him?"

Jed's eyes widened; his stomach began churning again. No one had asked HIM what to do with HIS dog! Standing as tall as he could and looking straight up into his friend's eyes, Jed said defensively, "Mistah Matt! Ya wouldn't want nobody to shoot ya 'cause ya broke your own leg, would ya?"

Matt gave Jed an impatient look. "He's just a stray, isn't he? Who needs a stray?"

Hanging his head, Jed shuffled his left foot across the floor — a habit he had whenever embarrassment overwhelmed him. Didn't Matt realize that he'd come to the fire station as a stray, too? His escape from the plantation, making his way north, the stench of some of the places where he had been forced to hide remained more than mere memories. When he'd finally arrived at the door of the Niagara Firehouse, he, too, had been no more than a tired, starving stray who felt unwanted — yet who had insisted they bed him down in the stable and let him work for his keep as a stable boy? MATT.

Why couldn't Matt catch the comparison? he wondered.

But as their eyes met, Jed realized he had. "Sorry, Jed, boy," Matt apologized once more, placing his hand on the former slave boy's shoulder. "I wasn't thinking – as usual. I always shoot off my mouth first and think later."

George joined the pair and chortled, "You said that right, Matt. If you opened your mouth any wider, you could stick your big foot right in."

Jed studied Matt's facial expression. Was he softening?

"All right, all right." A twinkle appeared in Matt's eyes. "If that fool dog's leg is broken, we need strips of cloth – and wood for a splint." Then trying to sound gruff, he ordered: "Don't just stand there gaping, Jed. Get them!"

Elated, Jed turned and began to run toward the stable, but stopped at the doorway. Looking back, his brown eyes softening, he said, "Mistah Matt...Mistah Matt, thank ya."

Matt responded in his best drill sergeant voice – the one that boomed out, seeming to begin down in the bottom of his oversized feet. "What are you standing there mumbling for, boy? How long do you want this dog to lay here and suffer?"

Maybe they would let him keep his dog! "No, suh, Mistah Matt," he hollered happily over his shoulder. "No, suh!" Grinning, Jed dashed out the door.

Chapter 2
Jack-in-the-Box

Running as swiftly as his long, lean legs would carry him, Jed arrived at his sleeping area in the corner of the stable. He hurriedly searched for the two thin pieces of wood he'd found a week or so earlier and stored in a cigar box, in hopes of whittling out a couple of funny animals. He'd already smoothed them down, so he knew they would make good splints.

Scanning the old stable, Jed wondered what they could use for straps to hold the splints in place on the dog's hind leg. His eyes always returned to his own small bundle of clothing. Since he could spot no clean rags or strips of cloth around, he picked up one of the two shirts he owned, gazing at it longingly for a brief moment. Then the boy hurried to the door, convinced he had the materials necessary to set the animal's injured leg.

At the stable doorway he paused briefly in thought, then looking behind him he retraced his steps to the pile of hay which was his mattress. Bunching it up in his arms, he gave a smug smile of satisfaction and headed back to the firehouse.

By the time he arrived, Matt had somehow carried the dog over to the large plank table the firemen had built so they could play cribbage during the long hours they sat on duty waiting for fire calls.

After Jed leaned down and placed the hay in a wooden box he'd made to carry the firewood for the firehouse stove, he walked over to Matt and handed him the two smooth sticks and his shirt. The fire chief looked at him quizzically and asked, "What you want me to do with this shirt, boy?"

Jed wished he'd taken time while he had been in the stable to tear the shirt into strips so he wouldn't have to explain. "Couldn't find nothin' fo' strips, Mistah Matt," he mumbled, "so I thought ya might's well use this ol' shirt of mine."

His big friend wrinkled his brow in disgust. "OLD shirt, ha!" Matt retorted. "You got two shirts to your name and you want to use one of 'em to bandage a stray mongrel!"

Matt shoved the shirt into Jed's middle with his right hand while his huge left hand fumbled with the buttons on the front of the one he was wearing. Before Jed could respond, Matt had stripped his own blue and white pin-striped shirt off his massive chest and with loud ripping noises tore it into strips.

Jed's eyes opened wide with surprise and alarm. "Mistah Matt! Mistah Matt!" he protested. "What ya doin' that fo'? How come you'se a-rippin' up yo' good shirt?"

Matt continued to make strips of cloth out of what only seconds before had been a very presentable shirt. "Ha!" Matt exclaimed. "You think you're special, or something? I'm the guy who kicked the dog – so I ought to furnish his bandage."

George, who had been standing by wordlessly watching their antics, shook his head and announced, "You're both crazy! The poor dog hasn't had any help yet because the two of you can't agree on anything. Matt, you're so busy tearing up your shirt, you forgot about the box of clean rags in that old dresser drawer." In an attempt at efficiency, George moved his tall slender frame between the two debaters. He motioned to Matt. "Now, you hold this dog down. And, Jed, you hold his mouth shut so he doesn't bite any of us when we hurt him."

In obedience Matt did precisely as he was told – with one of his large powerful hands he held the body of the fragile-looking animal very still. Jed was a little more cautious about his part in the operation. "Easy, boy, easy," he pleaded with the dog, knowing it might turn on him at any second. After he managed to encircle the dog's nose with his thin black hand, the dog whimpered, then relaxed. Jed breathed a sigh of relief.

"I'll be blessed, Jed," Matt declared with a tone of dismay. "You've got this fool animal under a spell. What did you do to make him your friend? I'm not one to go messin' around with no strange dog's mouth!"

A wistful smile passed over Jed's face as he thought of the candy and the times he'd spent alone with the dog before Matt had returned to work and the engine had come back to the fire station. Neither Matt nor the other firemen had any way of knowing his secretive befriending – that was just between him and the dog.

As George straightened the broken leg the dog wriggled slightly and gave a whimper. Jed watched as the muscles in George's thin white arms tightened beneath his skin. He felt beads of perspiration forming beneath his own dark curly hair. How he wished the operation was over!

George worked swiftly. Placing a piece of the smooth whittling wood on each side of the injured leg, his deft fingers wrapped the strips of Matt's shirt tightly around the splints to keep them from moving out of place.

Jed expected a reaction from the dog, but it didn't move or cry after the first whimper. Yet it seemed eternity passed by before George tied the final knot in place.

"There you are, fella," George told the animal. "I'm no dog doctor, but I'll bet your leg will soon be good as new."

Reaching down, Jed carefully lifted his animal friend, then carried him over to the wood box he'd filled with the hay from his own bed. "Here ya are, fella," Jed said soothingly. "Jes stay here and git better."

During the next few days, Jed watched over the dog in every spare moment, marveling at its determination to stand on its injured leg. Every day Jed managed to save the dog some food, but the weight it was gaining from those meager scraps puzzled him.

Something else amazed Jed, too – the dog never seemed ferocious or to even fear Matt's presence when he was close by. No matter how much the man who had kicked him grumbled, hollered or complained, the dog always perked up when Matt was near.

Didn't the dog remember that Matt was the one who had caused him all his pain and discomfort? He had been told of animals who had hated certain men all their lives because of such brutal acts. This dog appeared to be anything but stupid.

Because of his curiosity, Jed kept a watchful eye, but just couldn't find a clue to the close relationship developing between Matt and the dog – until one night when Matt was on duty by himself at the fire hall. Just past ten o'clock Jed wandered over to the firehouse from the stable, in hopes of getting the dog and taking him to bed with him. He enjoyed the dog's company – more than human companionship really. It seemed to understand Jed when he talked. The thing Jed like best about talking to his animal friend was that it always listened attentively and never answered back.

While walking past the fire hall window, Jed glanced at two shadowy forms inside. Because the light from the kerosene lantern was so dim, he retraced his steps to make certain he wasn't imagining the scene. He gaped in amazement. There sat Matt, big as ever, tenderly stroking the dog as it rested in his lap!

Jed suppressed a chuckle as he watched his large friend dip his wide hand into a brown paper sack, bring up a scrap of meat and offer it to the dog. This one glance into the firehouse window had solved two mysteries – why the animal was so fond of Matt and why the dog had been putting on weight.

As Jed turned to go back to the stable, the amusement he'd managed to suppress came out as a giggle, then increased to a loud chuckle. Matt had fooled everyone, including the former slave boy. Up until that time he'd been worried that the dog would lose his home as soon as his leg was healed, but that was beginning to look doubtful. If Matt was taken by the dog, no one else would dare suggest he must go.

Days passed and the dog's leg grew stronger. How comical it looked, hopping in and out of its wooden box with its leg still in a splint. Jed suspected Matt somehow had seen him at the window that night or had known he had been there, because he no longer put on any pretense about hating the dog when he was in Jed's presence. Often Matt reached down to pat the animal without caring whether or not Jed saw him. Not so with the other firemen, though – Matt continued to pretend the dog was a thorn in his flesh, talking gruffly to him when they were around.

For several weeks the firemen had been involved in a cribbage tournament. Plump, jolly Harry Svetland had jokingly bragged from the start, "I will be the next champion of the Niagara Volunteer Firehouse!"

Thus far no one had any real reason to dispute his proclamation, for Harry had defeated every man except youthful impetuous Tom Drysdale. Jed knew Tom would not give in easily, for he was one fireman who hated to be beaten at anything.

All the men had been anticipating the Friday night play-off, but when Tom came into the fire hall, speaking in a surly manner, one of the other men spoke to calm the young tousle-haired man. Jed wondered why he was carrying a chip on his shoulder. Was he that uptight about winning? From his seat at the cribbage table Harry called to him, "Hey, Tom, you ready to get massacred?" Tom's temper flared instantly and Jed feared there was going to be a duel instead of a cribbage game.

"Who do you think you are?" Tom demanded. To everyone's surprise he rushed toward Harry as if to punch him.

"Aw, Tom, can't you take a little jest?" Harry asked, easing the tension. Because of this episode an uneasiness pervaded the fire hall. From the start of the game all the men watched every move anxiously. Jed wished the tournament had never started – the usual congenial atmosphere was missing among the old firehouse gang. Jed noticed Matt, too, was watching with apprehension, for periodically he walked over to pet the dog.

Just when it looked as though Tom would go down in defeat, Matt sauntered by the wooden box and stroked the dog again. Harry glanced up from the heated game and burst into fits of laughter. Everyone turned from their concentration on the progress of the game to see what could have amused the boisterous fireman to such a degree.

Belligerent, Tom slammed his fist on the big wooden table and demanded, "What's so funny?" Harry continued to chuckle – his plump belly jiggling up and down with amusement. It was obvious to Jed that this was the first time Harry had seen Matt near the dog, for he cried with delight, "Matt! What are you doing, patting that 'stupid dog' – that 'canine curse'?"

Matt's face tinged pink, then burst into crimson. Turning his back to the men, he spat a wad of tobacco into the spittoon. Jed recognized this as an act to cover Matt's embarrassment. "Play your game, Harry!" Matt ordered. "Tend to your own business! What I do with this Jack-in-the-box is up to me!"

"That's it, Mistah Matt! That's it!" Jed cried out in excitement. "We cain't jes call 'im DOG fo'evah. He's bin a Jack-in-the-box fo' these las' few weeks – let's call 'im Dog Jack!"

Matt nodded in agreement and the two players resumed their game. Harry Svetland became jubilant as he moved his last peg to the end of the cribbage board, winning the contest. Tom hung his head and had little to say the rest of the evening.

"It's all right, Tom, lad," Harry mocked as he winked at Jed. "There were several things gained this night. I became the new Niagara Volunteer cribbage champ and Dog Jack seems to have found a new master, a new name and a permanent home."

Chapter 3
Sudden Manhood

Jed was so thrilled with Dog Jack's acceptance at the firehouse that he was unable to sleep that night. From his hay mattress he spent hours staring at the stable's rough-hewn ceiling and for some unexplainable reason the entire episode of the dog's arrival and acceptance caused him to dwell on his own roots and how he, too, had come as a stray to the Niagara Volunteer Firehouse. Because he had left his childhood home, Jed had suffered much loss – emotional and personal – but Matt and the other men had helped, in part, to fill in some of his lonely hours.

Now there was something that was his. Dog Jack belonged to him, was a part of him. For too long Jed had felt like a man without a country, without anything to call his own, but the animal helped occupy the void left when he'd been forced to run away from his family.

Sleepless, he stared wide-eyed at the knots in the ceiling overhead as every detail of the tragic days which caused him to flee from his family and friends whirled through his mind.

In his mind's eye he could still see himself in the twilight walking up to his family's rickety wooden shack on the far edge of Master Cooper's plantation in southern Virginia. He had reached up with his long, lean arms and with ease touched the top of the crooked unpainted door frame. Tired as he was, he forced a grin. How long he'd dreamed that someday he'd be able to reach that far without stretching – to Jed that was a sign of sudden manhood at the age of thirteen. Even though his body was bone-weary, he still felt he'd made a giant step in his young life.

Young Jed's thoughts were distracted when a voice from behind him spoke softly, "You'se 'most a man now, son." Turning, he looked straight into his father's eyes – something else he'd always hoped to be able to do.

In the dim light of sunset he saw his father flash a faint smile, but also sensed a touch of sadness in his Pappy Noah's voice. *Poor Pappy,* Jed thought. *Seems as though he's been feelin' right poorly lately. He looks so old at his young age.*

Jed had gone on in to bed. In the morning he was surprised to find he didn't feel much taller or grownup than he had the day before – no more a man than usual. With his mother and little sister, he walked down to the large field surrounded by tall cottonwood trees just as he had any other day.

As the morning progressed, he engrossed himself more and more with the rhythm of cutting the tobacco. The sun blazed down with fury. By mid-afternoon, Jed paused to wipe his brow, wishfully thinking, *If I could only have a break!* The thought had no sooner crossed his mind when Master Cooper himself walked over to the end of the row where Jed was working. "Jed, go to the storage shed and bring down more twine," he barked.

Jed was more than glad to oblige. His body had worked up such a sweat that his mouth and throat felt as dry as pods of cotton.

How he welcomed the shade of the big, old, cottonwood trees which lined the path from the field to the shed. For a moment he felt lighthearted – so pleased to get away from his usual daily drudgery. Then the sight of someone slumped against the trunk of a tree up ahead stopped him dead in his tracks.

Standing still for only an instant – it took his mind only that long to identify the bent figure – Jed rushed to the side of his father. Trying to hide panic from his voice, he leaned down and spoke in a soft voice, "Pappy? Pappy Noah?" Concern swelled within him. Why was his father so still? Why were his eyes so tightly closed?

When at last Pappy Noah glanced up, Jed was startled. Surely his father had aged ten more years overnight. "Pappy, can I help ya? Let me help ya," he urged, feeling more helpless and frightened than he ever had before.

His father spoke in little more than a whisper, "Go, go, Jed. You don't need to be fetchin' yourself no trouble. I'll be all right, son."

Disheartened, Jed stood up, weighing what his father had just told him to do. With great effort Pappy Noah lifted his arm to tell Jed to go on, and in a much firmer voice ordered, "Jed! I said, 'GO!' We don't have need of no more miseries!" Jed recognized his parent's no-nonsense tone, weak as it was, so he did his father's bidding. Reluctantly but obediently he continued on his way to the storage shed.

His Pappy Noah worked in the kitchen of Master Cooper's mansion and often left their shack to go fire up the stoves for breakfast before sunrise when the rest of the family went to the field. Jed had the highest respect for his father; for him Pappy was a pillar of strength and integrity.

Yet Jed's internal gnawing told him that continuing on his way was not what he should be doing. Mustering up strength to steady his quivering knees, he rushed to the storage shed, searched for a large role of twine, and returned to the path as quickly as he could. To his dismay his father was not where he had left him, nor was he anywhere in sight. He was not sure whether he should be sad or relieved about the situation, but knew for certain that he must inform his mother of the problem.

Back at the field, his small sister, Shadow, darted over to him. "Where's Mammy?" he inquired, managing to free a hand to fondly tug at one of her jet black braids in the hope of concealing his concern. With an impish and affectionate grin, she pointed to the far end of the same rows of tobacco between which she had been running. Dropping the twine to the ground, he headed in his mother's direction, his baby sister close at his heels as she usually was — the reason he had nicknamed her "Shadow."

"Mammy, Pappy's sick," he announce with alarm. Raising her hand, his mother hushed him before he could say more.

"I knows. I knows, son," she declared, looking around to see if any of the field bosses heard what Jed had said. "He'll be taken care of. Best ya git ta doin' yo' job again."

Reluctantly Jed went back to work as he had been told, but the uneasiness he felt about his father's well-being continued to haunt him. How grateful he was when the dinner bell finally rang, summoning the slaves from the fields for the day. Along with the other tobacco cutters, he trudged slowly past the Cooper mansion overshadowing the distant line of tumble-down sheds they all called home. More than ever before he noticed the weariness, a look of hopelessness in each of his co-worker's eyes.

As he neared the mansion path, Jed glanced up and saw two men carrying a still, human form out of Master Cooper's kitchen door. Horrified, Jed realized they were carrying his father! Forgetting his weariness, he ran up the stone path and arrived at the large brick structure just as the men neared the bottom of the spotless porch steps with their burden. Jed's eyes met those of old Mose, the chef, and Amos, his assistant. Mose's eyes looked down on the young out-of-breath lad with such concern and compassion that he knew without their telling him that his father was dead. Stunned, he stood hopelessly by and watched them carry his father's motionless body beyond the carriage house and out of sight.

Suddenly Jed's mother stood beside him. Silently she took in what was taking place. Then, unable to stifle her sorrow any longer, she heaved a huge sob. Despair hit Jed, too. At the moment his mother released her grief, the realization that he was fatherless hit him full force. He did not know whether to scream or cry, but quickly determined in his heart he should do neither, even if his grief-filled chest should burst. He was a man! Men did not do those sissy things. No, he would NOT give Master Cooper the satisfaction of seeing him break down. A surge of hate flooded his mind. Why hadn't Master Cooper given Pappy Noah the attention he'd needed when he had obviously become so ill? Why? Why? WHY?

At that moment Master Cooper strode up through the crowd of gathered slaves. Riding whip in hand, his voice boomed out with authority: "Nothing can be done now! Move on!" Silently the slaves slipped off into the twilight.

Master Cooper turned to address Jed. "You can build Noah a coffin out of the pine boards in the back of the stable if you want. Otherwise we'll just bury him in the ground in the morning."

Jed's mother turned to him as if to question whether he should tackle such a painful and emotional project after a hard day's work in the field. "I has ta do it, Mammy," he assured her. "Cain't have Pappy die and be put down in the ground with no coffin to bury 'im in."

He started toward the stable, glancing back to see his mother lean over and lift Shadow and cradle her in her tired, aching arms. Jed knew his mother well enough to realize that she was holding his baby sister close in her ample bosom, not only for Shadow's sake, but to console herself as well.

Since darkness was setting in, Jed lit a lantern and set it on an old barrel close to where he planned to work. Without asking permission, he began sorting through the pile of pine boards, taking the best he could find for his immediate need. The finest coffin he could build was the last tribute he could offer his father.

After locating a hammer and nails and a saw, Jed began to construct a box. Diligently he worked as the lights inside the great brick plantation house were lit. Music and laughter drifted through the air, causing resentment and bitterness to swell up inside him once more. How could the

Cooper family be in such a happy mood when his Pappy Noah, their long and faithful servant, had just died? Did white folks have no feelings at all?

His only consolation came from the sound of the negro spirituals drifting up the hillside until the words of one of the songs his fellow slaves were singing hit him with great impact. "Massa's in da col', col' ground." A wave of nausea swept over him as he thought about the fact that the pine boards he was hammering would soon become the box which would take his father to his earthly grave. "Pappy! Oh, Pappy!" he moaned. "Jes' yesterday ya was sayin' I'm 'most a man. Now I have ta fill your shoes. It don't seem fair! TAIN'T fair!"

Once he finished the pine box, he found two sticks suitable for making a cross-shaped grave marker. Surely his father deserved that much! Nails wouldn't hold the fragile wood, so he used a piece of baling twine to tie the sticks together and form a cross of sorts. Once he'd completed his project, he realized there was no way for him to let the world know for whom that marker had been fashioned. As a slave, he had never learned to read or write. Although over the years his father had learned a little bit about what he'd called "the three r's," Jed had never had a chance to learn anything of that kind.

Once more resentment swelled up inside him. He could not even print his own father's name – he simply didn't know how! Deprived of the freedom to grieve for his Pappy and deprived of the knowledge of how to read and write because he had been born and still remained a slave – never in his life had he experienced more inner turmoil. Somehow, someday, he would get back at Master Cooper for his unconcern for and neglect of his many slaves.

Chapter 4
Night Flight

HOW CAN I FACE THIS DAY? Jed thought when he opened his eyes. It had been in the wee hours of the morning when he'd finally finished the unpleasant task he'd begun the previous night. Just before dawn he'd been awakened as usual by the shuffling of his mother's feet as she moved about on the rough pine flooring of their cabin. Her moving about so early informed him that she had not slept well.

Hearing his stir, she spoke into the darkness, "Jed, Mastah Cooper said he was gonna perform the services jes' before we-all gets out on the field. Reckon ya best get up and dressed, boy." Jed moaned. "Mercy, chile, your bones mus' be achin'!"

For a moment Jed stretched lanky throbbing limbs and yawned, then with one deliberate push he was up and out of bed.

Trying to cheer his mother, he said, "I's fine, Mammy. Maybe all a body ever needs is an hour's rest or so."

After a breakfast of cold grits, Jed voiced his thoughts. "Mammy, who d'ya suppose fired up the cook stove this mornin'"?

With a shrug of her shoulders, she answered, "Old Mose or Amos, I 'spect. Don't worry, one of 'em did."

"I wasn't worryin', Mammy. Jes wonderin'."

Shortly after their brief conversation the bell pealed. It wasn't time to go to work, but Jed knew why Master Cooper was summoning them early. They had a most unpleasant task to do before they began their regular daily work load.

As the slaves walked toward the hillside, Jed trailed, making a point of staying close by his mother's side. Shadow followed close behind. How could he console his widowed mother? "Mammy," he asked, "do ya think Pappy's in heaven already?"

"Sho 'nuff do, son. Your Pappy didn't have a mean bone in his body and he had the greatest respec' fo' the Lord."

Jed and his mammy walked up the hill to congregate with the other workers already assembled in the small slave cemetery. All of Jed's brothers and sisters except Shadow were buried there. Many of them hadn't made it past birth. Their graves, marked by a line of seven little crosses in one section of the hillside burial ground, reminded Jed of the large family they could have had. Seeing that Jed and his mother had arrived, Master Cooper solemnly opened his Bible to a passage of scripture and handed it to Old Mose who seemed to be taken off guard by the gesture.

Glancing over the page, Mose started reading, "...In my Father's house...." Tears welled up in his eyes. Unable to read further, he turned to his master and pleaded, "Please, please, Mastah Cooper, don' ask me ta read the Good Book right now. I's jes' a-feelin' too poorly ta even try."

Master Cooper retrieved the Bible and finished reading the scripture Mose had begun. After that he prayed, "Lord, we give you Noah for safekeeping. Amen." The Amen had hardly left his mouth when he added in a loud and gruff tone of voice, "Time to get to work. You're already late starting."

Jes' like that! Jed thought. *He jes' put my Pappy Noah in the ground. Now he wants us back pickin' his 'backer again. Black men must not be human in white men's eyes!*

All morning, all afternoon he slaved in the scorching heat of the sun – just as he had every other day.

One Sunday a few weeks before he'd listened to Old Mose quote a verse of scripture: "There's a time to mourn." Didn't Master Cooper know that?

He remembered then how he'd been impressed by the words of a slave from a neighboring plantation. Having accompanied his master on a business call, the man, prematurely gray around the temples, had entered the storage shed where Jed and some of the others were working, looked around, then slid his thumbs under his twine suspenders and told them, "You folks jes' don't know what slavery really is. You got yo'self a good Christian mastah and can thank the good Lord in heaven for that! This is the only place I ever heard tell of where slaves hold church and have chicken dinnah come Sunday."

At the time Jed had considered himself most fortunate, but the happenings of the past few days caused him to wonder — what would it be like to be free and make decisions for your own life instead of having them made for you?

The same day as his Pappy's funeral he'd been given the task of driving the tobacco wagon up to the storage barn and hanging the bundles on the drying racks. Just as he was going out the back door to carry in his last load, he ran smack into Master Cooper's son Kirk. Jed tried to smile, grieved and weary as he was, for Kirk and he had been buddies since they were small. Still — lately Jed sensed that Master Cooper resented their friendship and would like it to discontinue.

Kirk, just three months older than Jed, extended his right hand, intending to offer consolation, and Jed understood that his friend was trying to say without words that he was sorry over Jed's loss. Seeing no response, Kirk asked, "Want to have a go-around with my marbles? Might help take your mind off your troubles."

"Cain't, Kirk. I still got more 'backer ta put away. Jes' 'magine what yo' pappy'd say if he ketched us playin' with them agates when I's still needin' to finish mah chores."

"Aw, come on, Jed," Kirk coaxed as he drew a circle in the dirt just outside the shed door. "Just one game. Work'll wait."

The battle of marbles had just reached a fever pitch

when Master Cooper strode up with his riding whip in hand. Neither boy saw him arrive; they were far too intense in outdoing each other in the game.

Jed had tossed his shirt aside early in the day, so his bare black back glistened in the late afternoon sun. Suddenly from behind came the crack of a whip and instantly Jed felt a piercing pain as the thongs made their mark.

"Ohh!" he moaned. Caught unexpectedly, he fell face down in the dust.

The whip found its target again — not just once, but seven times. Tears surfaced and smarted in Jed's eyes; he bit his lip to keep from crying out again. As the leather's final blow ripped and stung his flesh, Master Cooper's words brought an even deeper sting which cut into his very soul. "You stay away from my son, you NIGGER, you!"

Glancing up, he watched Kirk scramble to his feet and scurry away. Some friend, the one who'd coaxed him into the game! When trouble'd come — he'd turned tail and run away. Again bitterness surfaced inside Jed. Somehow he wanted to lash out at Kirk. Didn't he even care that he'd caused him such pain on the worst day of his life?

Master Cooper also left hurriedly. Jed knew he had to finish his chores even though the muscles in his back spasmed with pain and his skin smarted. He struggled to hang the last few bundles of tobacco leaves before heading toward his family cabin where his mother stood waiting in the doorway.

Jed tried to turn so she wouldn't spot the bruises on his bare back, but was quite sure that somehow she'd already heard what had taken place. Carefully, she reached out and turned him around so she could survey the damage. Without a word she picked up the chipped old basin and filled it from the water pitcher, then reached for a large pad of cotton. She spoke with tenderness, "Get down, son, so I can work on those wounds." Without looking at her face he knew she was next to tears.

Obediently Jed sprawled out on his lumpy mattress on the rough wood floor. While his mother dabbed gently at his wounds his pain sharpened, causing him to grimace and pull air in through his front teeth.

"Mammy!" he cried, "what ya got in that water? It smarts!"

"Jes' salt, Jed. Know it's gonna burn now, but it'll keep yo' sores from festerin' later."

Jed could feel sweat beads popping up all over his body as his mammy dabbed the salt solution across the open cuts from Master Cooper's whip. Once finished, she leaned down, tousled his hair and tenderly kissed his cheek.

Weariness from all he'd done physically, along with the emotional upheavals of that day, seemed to be too much to bear. His last thought before drifting off to sleep was one of despair. *If this is what it's like bein' a man, I don't knows if I want ta be one or not!*

Chapter 5
Unexpected Journey

The smarting stripes on his back, the sting of Master Cooper's words, the painful and disappointing rejection by Kirk, his lifelong friend, did not prevent Jed from sleeping soundly that night. Sheer exhaustion caused him to drift off into slumber as soon as he closed his eyes. He even forgot to say his prayers, something he'd always done as far back as he could remember. For several hours he slept sprawled out on his stomach in the same position he'd been in when his mother had tended to his wounds.

Unaccustomed to sleeping in that manner, he had tried to turn over in the middle of the night. "Ahh!" he moaned, the slightest movement feeling as though someone was stabbing him in the back. He came to his senses long enough to realize the cutting pain was caused by his wounds, then dozed off to sleep again.

Suddenly, awake and alert, he heard the familiar shuffle of feet on the wooden floor. *What now?* he wondered in the predawn hours. *Nothing else had better go wrong!* Those thoughts had hardly flashed through his mind when his mammy bent over beside his mattress and spoke gently. "Jed, Jed, son – ya hurtin'?" Although her face was not visible in the dark of the night, he sensed she was close to tears again.

Dropping down beside him on her knees, his mother then sat on the edge of the mattress of cotton she'd managed to make for him the night before. Tenderly she stroked his forehead as she spoke, "Now, son, ya gotta listen. I couldn't sleep a wink this livelong night, 'cause I's been a-worryin' about ya. Fo' some strange reason, it looks like Mastah Cooper's wantin' to make ya more trouble. Don't know if it's 'cause of yo' pappy dyin' or if he's jes' feelin' down right ornery and mean right now, but I knows I jes' cain't stand by and let somethin' happen ta you too. You and little Shadow's all's I got left in this world."

Wincing with pain, Jed raised his head. "Nothin's gonna happen to me, Mammy," he tried to reassure her.

"But, Jed boy..." Her voice rose in pitch and from experience Jed recognized that she was determined about what she was going to say. "Trouble's already happenin', son. If the mastah'd stand by and whip ya for playin' marbles with his own chile, what else he gonna do to ya?" She heaved a deep sigh, then began to sob, "He claims to be a Christian, but the good Lord knows he shoulda' been lookin' out better for his slaves. If he'd a got your pappy doctorin' and 'lowed him some rest, surely to heavens he wouldn't-a had ta leave us behind so early in life."

The bitterness which had subsided as Jed had fallen asleep surfaced inside him once more. "Don't talk 'bout it, Mammy," he advised his mother, carefully raising to a half-sitting position. "Jes' makin' me hurt on my insides and outsides all over agin. Besides, tain't nothin' I can do. Cain't even run away!"

"Yes! Yes ya can, Jed. I's been a-sittin' here a-thinkin'! Tain't no reason for to have to spend all yo' life with the miseries. Except for Shadow, all my other chilluns is already dead. I cain't take her and run with ya, 'cause we'd jes' slow ya down and we'd all be hunted and ketched and brought back here. We couldn't run fast enough, but ya'll can! You'se fast and strong!"

As the impact of her words began to sink in, Jed cried out in a hoarse whisper, "Mammy! You're thinkin' I should run away? Where'd I go? I's never been off this land or away from ya in all my born days!"

In spite of his restless urge to be free and think for

himself, the idea of leaving the security of familiar faces and places to run off into an unknown world was more than he could grasp, yet Jed knew from the determined tone of his mother's voice that she wasn't going to give up. "Yes, ya can, son!" she repeated. "Ya needs to get up and get a-movin' 'fore the sun comes up. Nobody gonna miss ya 'til we go to the fields. Use yo' strength and those long, lean legs and ya can be miles away 'fore folks even knows you'se gone."

Jed bolted upright. The sharp impact from his wounds didn't affect him nearly as much as what his mother was urging him to do. "Mammy, but where kin I go? I don' know nobody or nothin'!"

"Head north, Jed. Hear tell white folks up there don't treat black folks bad. Pennsylvania's s'posed to be a good place for runaways."

"Pennsylvania? That gots ta be miles and miles from here, Mammy! How's I ever gonna find it?"

Without bothering to answer, she lifted herself up from the mattress and walked over by the doorway. He arose and followed behind her, expecting her to change her mind. But she did not. Instead she whispered hoarsely, "Here's all I got in this world to give ya, son." Handing him a small tattered bag, she added, "This here's yo' pappy's shirt and pants. Now hurry and git yo' clothes on! Ya gotta leave soon — 'fore daylight. I put in a piece of corn bread I saved from Sunday dinner. All I got left to give ya is my prayers, Jed. No matter where ya find yourself, remember your mammy's prayers go with ya."

Dumbfounded, Jed stood as if in a daze for a moment before putting on his clothes. His mind whirled. He desperately wanted to stay, but his mother's persistent urging continued. "Jed, Jed — go find a better life. There's gotta be somethin' better for ya out there."

Before Jed could protest further, she placed the bag in his arms and headed him toward the open door. Once he'd watched an oriole shove her young from the nest and felt he was being pushed out in the same way.

For a moment they stood together in the doorway,

peering silently into the darkness. Then he thrust himself into his mother's arms. "Mammy, Mammy!" he whispered, longing to stay forever within the security of her grasp. The pain her hug aroused on his whip-beaten back didn't hurt half as much as the realization that this could be the last time he would ever feel his mother's embrace.

She permitted him to cling to her for a brief moment, then declared, "Don't make it no harder, Jed. Jes' go! Someday we should all be safe and free and together agin." She hugged her lean son close to her soft, plump body, then suddenly, as if she were afraid she would change her mind, she let go of him and spoke with determination, "Go, son! Go quickly...and God be with ya."

The last mother's touch Jed felt was a slight shove which turned him around and down the two wooden steps. He ran across the clearing toward a thicket of great oaks. At the edge of the trees he stopped to look back longingly at his family home which was little more than a shack. Somehow he felt as though he was living a dream. At such a young age how could he possibly leave all he knew and loved? As fear of the unknown flooded his body, his heart raced, pounding inside his chest. Would this be the last time he would ever see the place he'd called home? Who would take care of Mammy and Shadow, now that Pappy Noah was gone?

All he could make out in the moonlight was the silhouette of the cabin. He could not even see his mother standing in the doorway, but her frantic urging rang out across the night. "Hurry, Jed! Hurry, son!" With deep regret he turned to go.

Chapter 6
Mirror Image

Jed worked his way through the thicket – no easy task in the dark. Tree limbs scratched across his face. At one time he felt his right foot sink. His heart sank with it. He tugged and pulled to extract his foot out of the marshy spot. Unable to see the terrain around him, he chose to veer off to the left. Finding firm footing again, he decided his choice had been in good judgment.

Racing memories of the recent events and horrors of the past two days could have easily numbed his mind, but he refused to dwell on what he'd left behind. His main thought was to move on – to keep pressing forward as fast as he could.

Suddenly the forest he was stumbling through became visible, as if someone had lifted the dark shades of night. Streaks of gold glittered between the huge oaks. Dawn was painting its picture of early morning splendor, yet to Jed it was an ominous sign. Master Cooper would soon be aware that he was missing. Earnestly Jed hoped that the Coopers had stayed up late entertaining company the night before so Master Cooper would arrive in the fields later than usual. None of the slaves would ever report Jed missing – of that he was certain. Master Cooper would have to be informed by Jed's white overseer.

Suddenly Jed stopped short. He listened intently. Panic nearly overcame him. Did he hear dogs baying in the distance? No, he decided, and hurried on. Jed didn't have to guess what could happen if he were caught running away, for he'd witnessed one example. He cringed at the memory of the one slave who'd escaped not long after Jed had become old enough to work full days in the fields. The escapee had nearly made it to freedom, but Master Cooper had sent the hounds out after him. The man had come back in chains, blood oozing from the wounds where the dogs had attacked him as though he was an animal. His overseer had made a spectacle of him before the other slaves to discourage the rest of them from running away.

Jed thought, *No one else dared leave — until now!*

Minutes of running became hours. He reached a clearing just as the sun shone brightly overhead. At the thicket's edge he paused, taking time to reach into the cloth sack his mother had packed and pull out the piece of golden corn bread which had drastically diminished in size during the journey.

Licking his fingers generously, he stuck them deep into the corners of the sack to retrieve every crumb he could find. How he relished the taste, even though it didn't begin to satisfy his hunger or his thirst.

As he struck out once again across the open field, the blazing sun caused him to break into a heavy sweat. After tramping through acres of green pasture land where no one noticed him except a few brown and white cows who eyed him inquisitively, he spied a farmhouse in the distance. Off to the right he noticed a low, shed-like building and decided it would be an excellent place in which to take shelter from the heat of the afternoon, rest his weary legs and smarting wounds and perhaps even find some kind of nourishment.

Nearing the shed, he crouched down lest anyone from the brown clapboard house might be looking in his direction. Glancing about as he neared the door of the shed, he could see no one in sight. The hinges on the large old wooden door creaked as Jed opened it. His heart fluttered. The noise had announced his arrival! Once inside, his presence sent a flock of chickens squawking into the air, feathers and chickens flying wildly around him.

A chicken coop! Master Cooper had one of his own, but Jed had never been inside. Even though Jed froze, statue-like, it seemed an eternity before the big birds ceased to flutter and make noises of alarm because of their intruder.

Hungry as he was, Jed knew his conscience would never let him steal a chicken. Just thinking about it he could hear his mammy's voice in his mind: "Land o' mercy, boy! Good folks nevah do such things." Yet he wondered if the good Lord wouldn't forgive him if his major theft in life was an egg or two. With determination he reached out to shoo the flock of protesting hens off their roosts once more so he could gather some of their eggs, but was interrupted by a thud in a separate room. *What was that?* he wondered and dropped to his knees. Crouching as low as he could, he waited motionless. Hearing no further noises, he thought, *Maybe somethin' fell.* Even so, he decided he should investigate with caution. Slowly and carefully he crawled on his hands and knees toward the partition.

About halfway to the wooden wall, he stopped. Did he hear something again? Pausing a few moments, he decided his imagination was going wild, so he started to inch forward once more.

When Master Cooper's runaway slave reached the end of the partition, he paused again, then slowly peeked around the corner. To his amazement, he found himself peering into a dark face with a set of brown eyes much like his own. The other lad was also in a crouched position. For Jed it was almost like staring at a mirror image of himself. Too startled, neither he nor the other boy spoke at first. Then Jed gathered his wits about him and exclaimed with a quiet chuckle, "Well, I'll be!"

Jed scrambled to his feet. Almost simultaneously the other boy also rose from his knees. Even when standing the two were nearly the same size. Jed extended his hand. "Name's Jed," he whispered. "What ya doin' heah?"

The other lad's eyes lit up as his mouth spread into a wide grin. "Mine's Eli. Guess I could ask ya the same thing – what ya doin' on yo' knees on some stranger's chicken coop floor?"

His question relaxed Jed enough to chuckle. "Nevah bin heah befo'. Never 'spect ta pass this way agin. I'se runnin' away from Mastah Cooper's plantation in Virginia."

The boy who had introduced himself as Eli sighed heavily, "You'se a-goin'; I'se a-comin' back."

"What ya mean?"

"I got word my pappy's sick to dying', so I'se goin' back ta the plantation. Runned away two years ago."

Wide-eyed, Jed stared at his new friend. The wounds on his back still smarted, especially since he had broken out in a nervous sweat. "Do ya know what they'se goin' ta do to ya?"

"Reckon they'se gonna beat me some more, but they nevah beat a good slave hand to death. They wants all the free help they can git."

"Where'd y'all come from just now?" Jed inquired.

Eli leaned against a post, pulled a piece of straw from between the boards of the partition and stuck it between his front teeth. "Pittsburgh. White folks treated me right fine up there. Kept me and paid me fo' mah work."

All those benefits sounded too good to be true, so Jed asked, "Where's Pittsburgh?"

"Pennsylvania."

"Pennsylvania!" Jed cried with delight. "My mammy said I should go to Pennsylvania, but I don't knows how to git there."

"You can hop a train. I'll show ya where to git it. There'll be one passin' north out of the freight yard jes' 'bout a mile from here later this afternoon. I's gonna be headin' to the yard too, but I need a train goin' south toward Baltimore."

"How'll I know which one to catch?" Jed inquired, excited yet unsure about the adventurous possibility of riding a train. "I nevah learned to read, so I don't wants to hop the wrong one and go south again." He leaned against the partition looking at the boy with whom he had so much in common. How he wished he could coax him into going north along with him. "Why ya want to go back and be a slave? Ya sure ya wouldn't like to come with me?" For the life of him, he couldn't imagine going back.

"I can read well enough to pick out the right train for ya," Eli answered. "I tol' ya – my pappy's dyin' and I's only gonna have one father in mah whole lifetime." Tears welled up in his eyes. "HAS ta go back – no matter if they whip me, beat me or put me in chains. I still has ta see my pappy one more time befo' he's gone. ...Reckon you're havin' a hard time understandin' how I feels."

Remembering the recent loss of his own father, Jed fought back the tears surfacing in his own eyes. He paused to gain composure before he spoke. "I ran away jes' after mah own pappy died."

Eli's face clouded with concern. "Then ya would understand, Jed. I's sorry. I'd be most happy ta help ya find your way north, but right now I have ta take care of mah biggest problem – I feel like I's starvin' half ta death!"

"Me too!" Jed agreed. "But I's not one to ever be no chicken thief."

"Me neither," Eli declared. "But ya don't 'spose the farmer would mind if we helped ourselves to a few eggs, do ya?"

"Raw?" Jed had never eaten such a thing.

"Sure, raw! They're mighty tasty when you're sufferin' from the hunger miseries."

Paying attention to nothing but their gnawing hunger, the boys shoved some hens aside, causing another great commotion. Amidst the clucking and scolding they reached under the flapping hens and retrieved three eggs apiece. Jed had just cracked one open and mustered up the nerve to sample the thick yellow liquid inside when the door burst open.

Jed and Eli dove for the rough dirty floor boards. From their poor vantage point they looked up at the barrel of a sawed-off shotgun. A towering bearded farmer in coveralls stared down at them.

Motionless, the two boys remained sprawled out on the floor, both too frightened to move a muscle.

"What in thunderation...?" the farmer asked. "I come out here to see what wild animal of prey's causing my hens to be in such an uproar, and here I find a couple of runaways stealing my egg supply."

We're in for it now, Jed thought. But to his surprise, the farmer dropped his shotgun to his side. "Come on, boys. You're a couple of lucky ones. You just so happened on a man who's sympathetic to your cause. One thing you need to know, though – my neighbors don't share my sentiments. We'd have a real hassle if they knew I harbored a couple of black runaways – so don't cross the next farm. They're apt to shoot you on sight."

Still trembling, the two boys waited for the farmer's next comment. "I know you're hungry. I need the chickens, but I'll manage without a few eggs." He turned and walked slowly back to the door where he paused. "I'm serious about you getting out of here right soon. I don't agree with my neighbors, but I want to live peaceably beside them."

Both boys shook their heads in agreement. The farmer asked, "You two brothers?"

"Oh, no," Jed answered. "We jes' met."

"Well...," the man drawled, "sure could be brothers – maybe even twins. Remember what I told you," he called over his shoulder as he walked away.

"Yes, suh! Thank you, suh!" the boys called enthusiastically in unison, then turned to each other and grinned. Suddenly both lads found themselves in each other's arms – laughing hysterically from sheer relief.

Moments later they quickly sobered up. "Bes' we git our eggs and be on our way," Eli advised.

"Sure 'nuf," Jed agreed. "We done promised."

Cracking open three more eggs apiece, they hungrily downed the contents. Jed pulled his father's shirt out of his cloth sack and put it on a wooden counter.

"Whatcha doin'?" Eli asked.

"Gonna take some along for the road," he explained as he carefully wrapped four eggs in the tail of the shirt.

"Good idear," Eli assented. He, too, wrapped and deposited four in the sack he was carrying.

"Bes' we git movin' on," Jed told his companion.

Eli nodded affirmatively. The duo quickly moved toward the chicken coop door. Jed's new friend hesitated for a moment before moving out into the open field. "We bes' be careful. We's already bin warned how the neighbors feels about black folks — but we gotta hurry or you'll be missin' yo' train."

Jed thought about their parting company; each would be all alone again. "Eli, wish ya was goin' along with me to Pittsburgh."

His friend nodded in wistful agreement, but said nothing. They started out across the neighboring fields of grain, both very much aware that their lives were at risk.

Chapter 7
Long Journey

While crossing the adjoining property, both young men crouched down low until the railroad yard came into view. A train whistled in the distance. "That one's comin' from the south, Jed! You'se in luck! We jes' made it heah in time fo' yo' train."

"Wha's we need ta do now?"

"We gotta hide till they change cars. Confounded bounty hunters swarm all over this heah place like a passle of bees sometimes. We bes' keep a sharp lookout. When the coast is clear, ya hops aboard an empty car. With any luck, ya'll fin' yo'self ridin' right smack into Pittsburgh. Tain't the safes' way, but it's the fastes'. The Unnerground Railroad the Quakers set up is the bes'. They hides ya down unner hay piles and moves ya from one mill to another in their buggies. They's good, kind Christian folk who'd risk their own skins to he'p darkies like us. Hear tell they go so far to protect the slaves they have ya walk on a plank so's ya never touch the groun'. After ya move on, they scrub that plank with lye so's no dog kin sniff ya out."

Jed felt uneasy. Why was he risking getting caught on the railroad? Hesitating for just a moment, he decided his friend had considered all the risks and had determined it was safe enough to try the train. Instead of protesting the plan as he'd first intended, Jed asked, "Where's we gonna hide?"

"Over here!" Eli ran to an area where railroad cars were

parked and hoisted himself up between two of them. Standing on top of the couplings, he leaned down and extended a hand to Jed.

Jed realized they could be spotted easily, standing in the open like they were. "Won' somebody see us here?"

"We's safe long's there's no bounty hunters 'round. Most a the folks workin' this yard knows slaves try ta use this spot ta hop freight trains goin' north. No skin off their noses – why should they care?"

Before Jed could respond, a train let off steam as it came to a halt on the track beside them.

"Yo in luck fo' sure," Eli assured him. "Jes' scoot over to that track right beside us real quick."

Jumping off the coupling he and Eli had been sharing, Jed immediately grabbed hold of a metal bar and hoisted himself up to the partially open doorway of a cattle car. He could see Eli watching from his vantage point. Jed wanted to holler across, to communicate with the friend he was leaving behind, but Eli put his finger to his lips, signaling him to be quiet.

Hearing footsteps in the slag along the track, Jed crouched low in a dark corner. A bounty hunter? He heaved a sigh of relief as he watched a railroad worker walking between the two trains, but remained out of sight until he was certain the man had passed by. Peering around the corner, he observed that the coast was clear. The engine hissed; the wheels began to clank, then slowly roll down the tracks.

The two boys' eyes met as they passed one another. So many thoughts raced through Jed's mind – things he knew he would never be able to share with Eli who waved a reassuring farewell. Wistful, Jed waved in reply. Just as swiftly as he'd come into Jed's life, his friend was gone.

Dejected, tired and lonely, Jed settled down against the wall of the freight car. Gratitude filled his heart because the door remained partially open. Otherwise he wondered if he would have been able to tolerate the unpleasant odor the cattle had left behind. His nostrils burned.

He placed the cloth sack his mother had given him behind his head for a pillow to lean against and gingerly leaned his tender back against the filthy wall. What was the crackling noise he heard inside the sack? Then he wailed, "Mah eggs! How could I forgit 'bout 'em?" Upon opening the sack and examining the contents, he found an expected yellow squishy mess inside his father's shirt. He wanted to cry.

After removing as many pieces of the shattered egg shells as he could, Jed sucked at the gooey spot until most of the yellow disappeared – relishing the nourishment, for he had no idea when he would eat again.

His bone weariness soon got the best of him and the rhythm of the swaying boxcar lulled him to sleep. Awakening from his fitful slumber once when the train came to a stop, he realized that night had fallen. Too exhausted to care, he promptly fell back to sleep.

Later he was awakened again by the sound of hissing steam. The brakes emptied of air and the train came to a halt.

As Jed tried to move from his leaning position, every bone in his body screamed in protest. His neck felt as though it had been twisted into knots, the wounds on his back stiff and sore. How long had he been riding – days? hours? He had no way of knowing how much time had passed, nor did he know where he was.

Peering outside the cattle car, he found unfamiliar sights. Ladies and gents wearing fine apparel bustled about. Horses pulling fancy black buggies trotted by.

For a moment he stood in the doorway, longing to cling to something – anything – he'd been accustomed to. Glancing at his sack, he noticed the sick-looking yellow spot had dried. He slung the cloth bag over his shoulder and lowered himself over the side of the car.

Unsure of himself, he sauntered into the mainstream of the milling crowd ahead. Scanning the faces, he hoped that at least one might be dark-skinned, but found none. Not one!

Finally he built up courage enough to ask a young boy who looked to be about his age, "Kin ya tell me where I am?"

"Sure, boy. Pittsburgh, Pennsylvania." Then nodding his head in the direction of a long wooden building, the lad added, "That's the railroad station."

How could he have been so fortunate as to have the freight train deliver him right where he wanted to go? *What a stroke of luck!* he thought, then remembered his mother was back home on the plantation praying for his safety.

A few people turned to stare at him as he walked along the busy street. Jed was aware his presence had become a conversation piece. Sack in hand, he turned down a less traveled cobblestone road.

From out of nowhere a large wagon pulled by two well-groomed but frothing horses raced down the road. A huge, red-faced man screamed from up on the driver's seat, "Get outa the way! You wanna get killed?"

Jed leaped out of the way just as the red wagon sped past. *Where could he be going in such an all-fired hurry?* he wondered, wishing he could read the words painted on the side. Immediately his mother came to mind and he thought, *Some place ya sent me to, Mammy! First thing tries ta do is run me over! Where's I gonna go an' what's I gonna do now I found Pittsburgh?*

After his near disaster, Jed was more cautious and watchful. *Where am I going and what am I to do, now that I'm in Pittsburgh?* were the two questions paramount on his mind.

Reaching a street corner some distance away from the railroad station, he stopped and inquired of an older man dressed in a distinguished looking business suit, "Kin ya tell me where I is now?"

"You're on the corner of Penn Avenue. That's the fire house over there," he answered politely, pointing to the west.

Since Jed had no notion of where he should go, he decided the firehouse would be as good a place as any. As he strolled hesitantly across the stone-covered drive, he heard a familiar voice bellow from behind him! The hair on Jed's arm stood on end. Of all the people in the world, why did he have to run into the same big bully twice in one day?

"Ho!" the man yelled at his team of horses, causing them to come to an abrupt stop right beside the runaway slave. As Jed jumped aside to make sure he wouldn't be hit, the huge man holding the reins demanded, "Boy, what you doin' here?"

Having no notion of what to say, Jed simply stood in meek silence, looking up at the wagon driver.

"Cat got your tongue?"

"No, suh."

"Oh, you can talk, can you?" the large man asked as he got down from off the wagon. "Name's Matt." He reached out and shook Jed's hand. "I'm the fire chief. I didn't mean to be so rude back there when I nearly ran you over, but I was in a mad rush to get to a fire. Now, I've told you all that – what's your name, son? Where you been?"

Jed wished the stranger hadn't asked, but he was certain this big bruiser would never be content unless he knew it all.

"Name's Jed. I's runnin' away from Mastah Cooper's plantation in Virginia. My mammy says white folks is kind ta black folks in Pennsylvania – so heah I is."

The fire chief's mouth dropped open. "Virginia's a long, long way from here, but your mammy's right. Most of us don't believe in slavery, young fellow. Where you planning to stay and how you going to eat, now you're here?"

Embarrassed, Jed shuffled his feet across the cobblestones. "I – don' know, suh," he admitted. "Don' have nobody or nothin' in these heah parts."

Matt grinned and placed one of his big arms across Jed's shoulders, causing Jed to think of David and the giant Goliath he'd heard about from Old Mose. "Wrong, son," Matt corrected him. "You got a friend. You got me! Had any supper?"

"No, suh."

"No breakfast nor dinner either, I reckon. Come on, boy, you need something that'll stick to your ribs."

Inside the fire station Matt got out a bread board and cut off two thick slices of bread, then reached inside a cupboard and pulled out a jar of strange looking stuff. After dipping a knife into a thick, lumpy dark red substance, he began to spread it across the bread.

"What ya puttin' on theah, Mistah Matt?"

"MISTER Matt?"

"Yes, suh. My mammy always tol' me anyone older than me deserves ta be called Mistah. Matter o' respectin' mah elders."

Matt gave him a half grin. Humor pranced in his eyes. "Trying to make an old man out of me, boy?"

"Oh, no, suh!"

"I'm just pulling your leg, Jed. Here, eat your bread and jam." Pushing the plate over toward him, Matt added, "It's right good eating. My Molly made it."

Jed lifted the bread with its topping to his mouth. Smacking his lips together, he declared, "Sure 'nuff tastes good! What ya call this stuff?"

Matt's eyes twinkled with amusement. "Strawberry jam," he answered. "You never had any before?"

"No, suh."

"Well, eat hearty!" Matt exclaimed as he shoved the bread board and jar of jam toward him.

"Eat all I wants?"

"All you want. Molly has more at home for us."

Jed clung to Matt's words. "For US? – do that mean I kin stay heah?"

"Don't see why not. Not afraid of work, are you, boy?"

"Heaven sakes, no!"

"Then I reckon you can have a job as stable boy. You can bed down in the hay up in the loft and you can eat with us. We've got a cook stove and the men on duty fix all their meals here."

"Don't have no money to pay ya," Jed sighed.

"Listen here, boy! We're against slavery. You do your job well and you'll earn your room and board. Later we might be able to give you some pay."

Wide-eyed, Jed stared at him. The man who'd frightened him so had turned out to be his first benefactor – a place to sleep and food for his stomach – even something tasty called strawberry jam. How lucky could a runaway slave be?

Chapter 8
Rumors of War

Jed soon fell into the routine of cleaning the stable, watering and feeding the horses and working around the fire station. He got used to the firemen and loved to stand by and hear them bicker between themselves during the many cribbage games which they played during their waits between fire calls. George Brown looked up from one of his games with Matt and spied Jed watching intently as they moved their pegs around the board.

"Jed, you want to play sometime?" he asked.

Jed shuffled his feet uneasily as he hung his head. "Cain't, suh."

Matt interrupted his play. "You can too, boy! We don't expect you to work all the time. We're not running a slave plantation!"

Jed was even more embarrassed. He had to explain, "Ya don't understand, Mistah Matt. Cain't read – not even numbers."

"Well, someday we'll have to fix that!"

Yet Matt never mentioned teaching him to read again, so Jed just kept busy working and watching and wishing somehow he could be part of the fun. One night just before falling asleep in the hay loft, he thought, *After all,* ya *may not be able to read and write, but ya's better off than any slave* boy *ya's ever known!*

Time had helped heal the deep cuts on his back and his

homesickness. As he became more and more involved with the firemen, he had fewer hours to dwell on missing Shadow and his mammy. The surprise party for his fourteenth birthday and the gift of candy from the firemen had made him feel he was very special to the men at the firehouse. Matt had taken him to parades and harness races. Dog Jack's arrival and companionship helped fill the terrible void he had experienced when he first came.

During those happy months at the firehouse, Jed heard rumors of wars. Since he could neither read nor write, he had to depend on the men for all his information. Surely Mr. Lincoln had to be the greatest man on earth. From listening to the firemen he heard how the President wanted to free the slaves. Matt and Tom talked about "emancipation" and "abolition." Jed wasn't sure about the meanings of those two big words, but if they meant freeing the slaves – he was all for them and for Mr. Lincoln.

Yet somehow Jed couldn't imagine himself going off to war. As much as he would have liked to have his mother and sister free and with him, he couldn't envision himself taking on the role of combat soldier to bring that dream to reality.

Matt obviously had a different opinion. Back in April, when full scale war had seemed imminent, he had declared, "The Rebs fired on Fort Sumter. President Lincoln has made an urgent appeal – seventy-five thousand state militia men. We need to volunteer together. We need to join up now and get those slaves set free! Sooner or later we're going to have to go to war anyway."

Jed was greatly relieved that few of the firemen shared Matt's zeal. How could he stand by and actually watch men's blood gush forth and flow down their bodies as he had seen in newspaper pictures?

During his growing-up years Jed had hated all white men – all except Master Cooper's son Kirk. As young boys Kirk and he had done many things together until Master Cooper had found them playing marbles together behind the storage barn and Jed had felt the dreadful sting of the plantation owner's whip.

He would never forget Master Cooper's seething rage, nor his words which still tore at Jed's heart: "You stay away from my son, you NIGGER, you!" It was difficult for Jed to discern whether the whip or the words had bruised him more. That day when Kirk had walked away, totally ignoring him in his pain and disgrace, Jed experienced deep hurt. Disillusioned, he had decided the son who had once claimed to be his friend was no better than the father.

Jed continued to despise all white men until he had come to the Niagara Firehouse where the firemen had taken him in and treated him as a human being. Because of this experience of acceptance he began to wonder – was he capable of killing anyone as he had once thought he could, or did he even want to? He had Dog Jack and Matt and the firemen. He was content with his life as it was. Sometimes Jed would lay in the hay mow which had become his bed in the firehouse stable, trying to relive in his mind life as it had been back at the plantation. He had difficulty thinking about his mother, his baby sister, Shadow, and the misery that must still be theirs.

Life moved on at a mundane pace until the memorable day of July twenty-first, eighteen sixty-one, when Matt came running into the firehouse waving a newspaper and crying out – "There's been a battle at Bull Run! We lost!"

Matt spread the newspaper out on the plank table while everyone gathered around. Jed wished then that he could read – all he knew by sight were a few numerals, so he had to piece together the bits of conversation in order to find out what was going on.

After a sigh of disgust, Matt exclaimed, pointing to the front page headlines. "Look at that, will ya! McDowell's army was winning and just when it looked like we could march right on into Richmond and wipe them out those Johnny Rebs brought in a second army! Look at the losses

— 481 killed, 1,011 wounded!"

From the shocked look on their faces Jed knew the other men were amazed that the North had suffered a defeat. George was the one to confess his confusion, "I don't get it. We've got more factories, more money, more people and more crops — and the South makes us turn tail and run!"

Several weeks later Jed stood just inside the firehouse door and watched a government man tack up a poster outside on the front wall. The poster, most impressive and patriotic, was a picture of Lincoln, an American flag and a bald eagle with its wings spread wide. Jed waited impatiently for Matt to arrive at work and read its message aloud, but to Jed's disappointment he read it silently, then started to walk away. Unable to contain his curiosity, Jed asked his large-framed friend, "What's it say, Mistah Matt?"

Matt glanced at him with a look of concern. "Well, I'll be! You don't know, do you? Someday I'm gonna teach you how to read, boy. It says here they'll give each of us two hundred twenty-five dollars if we'll join the Pennsylvania Volunteers. That's just for signing up, but they'll also provide us good food, clothes and take care of our families — and throw in twenty-five dollars a month to boot!"

Jed whistled a shrill whistle of amazement. "Phew! That's a lotta money and a lotta big promises!" he acknowledged with surprise. "Ever'thing a body needs!"

"Yeah," Matt mused, "worth thinking about."

During the ensuing days little attention was given to the always ongoing domino and cribbage games, for time was filled with talk about latest developments of the war and the government offer. Those were days of anxiety for Jed — any thought of going off to fight a war sickened him. He couldn't imagine getting up enough courage to kill any man. He didn't hate anyone anymore. Time had taken the bitterness out of his heart and it felt good. He didn't want to feel bitter and vengeful ever again.

Dog Jack was the only thing that seemed to make any of the men smile during this crucial and tense time of decision-making. His leg on the mend, he hopped in and out of his box, following after the men and obviously feeling he was part of the crew. As Jed now had a sense of belonging, so Dog Jack seemed to realize he'd found a home.

When Jack's leg had finally healed completely, with a little coaxing from Jed he learned to prance around the firehouse on his hind legs. His antics delighted the men who always begged, "More, Jack, more!" The dog obviously enjoyed performing, especially since the firemen always rewarded him with a morsel of food after each trick.

In the early part of August, Jed sensed tension growing as the firemen's anxieties about the war news increased. He shuddered as he thought how much the war could affect his small but comfortable world inside the fire station.

"Just imagine," Harry exclaimed as the men sat around the cribbage table one evening. "The kind of money the government offers could pay off all our debts and give our families a nest egg to live on. Two hundred and twenty-five dollars is more money than we see around here in four full months! Maybe we ought to sign up now before they quit paying so much."

"Yeah," Matt agreed. "They'll probably make us go sooner or later anyway, so we might as well get the best of the pay."

Such chatter unnerved Jed. None of his friends appeared to have a bit of concern about Mister Lincoln's war – about America, slavery or anything except the money and the excitement of fighting. Jed saw greed and glory mirrored in their eyes.

That afternoon while he and Matt were cleaning outside the firehouse he finally found the courage to ask, "Don't ya care 'bout the slaves, the United States of 'merica or 'bout nothin' else but the pay, Mistah Matt?"

Matt's grin transformed to a frown. "'Course I do, boy.

Do you think all the money in the world could make me leave my Molly behind to fight a war I didn't believe in?"

Jed's mouth dropped open. Why would his friend say such a thing? Molly was Matt's bride of only six months, but Jed had never seen two people who seemed to enjoy squabbling with each other as much as those two. That very morning Molly had stormed into the fire station, her green eyes blazing as she proclaimed for all to hear: "You big, dumb Swede! You spend money like you owned a gold mine! What do you mean looting my sugar jar?"

Matt yelled back to her, "YOUR sugar jar – but MY money! What money did you ever earn?"

Eyes flashing, Molly stood shaking her fist as she proceeded with her tongue lashing, but Jed could see Matt was beginning to soften. It always tickled Jed to watch how easily Matt always succumbed to Molly's fiery temper. The big, usually boisterous fireman suddenly hunched his shoulders and said softly, "Now, Molly, sugar, don't fret. I'll put it back next pay."

With the assurance of Matt's promise, Molly had turned and stomped out the door in a huff – steaming like a locomotive on the Pennsylvania Railroad.

Jed had thought then, *POOR MATT* – and was dumbfounded at Matt's not wanting to leave "MY Molly" to go to war. Evidently Matt didn't think he was "poor" at all!

As Jed continued to think about this puzzling marriage relationship, Dog Jack suddenly sprang to his feet from his bed in the wood box and began to bark. Their attention diverted by their canine protector and mascot, Matt and Jed both looked up to see what had aroused the dog.

A young boy raced toward them. Jed recognized the lad as Jimmy Malloy, the oldest of the thirteen children who all bore the family trademark of red hair and a bridge of freckles spanning each of their upturned noses.

Jimmy cried out, "Sound the bell! Sound the bell! Our

house is on fire!"

Jed turned to tug the rope to summon the firemen from the fields and various other places of work. Matt immediately turned to race toward the stable and fetch the horses. Dog Jack ran behind him, barking excitedly at his heels. Dog Jack always accompanied the men on their fire calls and knew something exciting was about to happen again.

Jed stood for a moment before deciding the best way to help was to follow Matt and help him hitch up the horses.

"Hurry! Hurry!" Matt ordered. "That fire must be well on its way by now! It took some time for that boy to get here on foot!"

As Matt jumped up into the driver's seat of the fire wagon, Dog Jack leaped up beside him. Matt raised the reigns, then hollered at Jed, "Come on, boy, come on – you might as well help with this one!"

Jed's heart leaped with anticipation – this was the first time Matt had offered to take him along! With one mighty jump he sprang up on the front seat, just as Matt cracked the whip over the horses' heads.

"Hang on!" Matt cried. Jed grabbed for Dog Jack when the wagon nearly toppled as it sped around the corner.

The horses had hardly gained momentum before Matt brought the wagon and team to a screeching halt. Volunteers raced from all directions. Jed found it difficult to hang onto Dog Jack who was jumping wildly and barking with enthusiasm at the men running toward the fire engine.

"Look at 'im, Mistah Matt," Jed declared, "he's tryin' ta tell 'em ta hurry up!"

Matt grinned in agreement. "Yep, he does everything BUT talk!"

In seconds the firemen were aboard and Matt once more cracked the whip. As they raced down the road, flames brightened the horizon and Jed feared the firemen were arriving too late to save the rambling old Malloy homestead.

When the wagon pulled into the Malloy property, the

firemen found the yard filled with spectators – people standing idly by, doing nothing but watching the black smoke and the crackling flames lick the back of the building.

Matt's face was flame red, but Jed knew it was not because of a reflection from the fire.

"Hang on, Jack! Matt's 'bout ta blow!" he cried as he reached to grab the dog by the collar.

At that very moment Matt swung down from his perch and, taking on his role as fire chief, bellowed in his best drill sergeant roar, "What are you standing there gaping for? Grab these buckets and line up! If you were any kind of neighbors, you'd have had this blame fire out by now!"

Matt threw his arms up in disgust just as Malloy's big shepherd watchdog bristled and, giving a low, throaty growl, leaped toward Matt – an involuntary reaction to the huge man's quick movement. Matt was too furious to hear or pay any attention.

"Get with it!" he commanded his own firemen. As he turned to reach for two buckets up on the wagon, the dog sprang toward Matt's throat with his jaws open wide.

Startled and caught off guard, Matt lost his balance, sprawling across the lawn with the huge shepherd on top of him. With one ferocious growl the dog missed his mark, sinking his front teeth into Matt's chest.

Jed remained frozen to the wagon seat, staring wide-eyed and helpless as blood oozed out of the wounds where the dog's teeth had been. What could he do to distract the savage beast?

Before Jed could think further, Dog Jack leaped from the fire wagon down onto the back of the attacker. Jed's stomach churned. The huge animal dwarfed Jack – it must have been twice Jack's size and weight!

Horrified, Jed stood by helplessly as the dogs rolled over and over across the lawn. Fur flew. The two dogs looked like one massive blob of fur and blood as the shepherd fought to release Jack's hold on his back. Their growls made the hair on Jed's arms stand on end. His heart pounded against his chest.

"Hang on, Jack, hang on!" Jed cried just as Matt rolled free and leaped back to his feet while roaring, "Get those buckets filled and get moving!"

Matt paused only long enough to pull a red handkerchief from his pocket, dab at his wounds for a second, then ran to join the bucket brigade.

What was Matt doing? Was he so calloused he didn't care about the Firehouse mascot which had just done battle on his behalf? Dog Jack had warded off a savage dog and possibly saved Matt's life, but Matt did nothing for Jack who was still in real danger. Jed simply could not understand that man!

One mighty shake of the shepherd dog's body caused Jack to lose his tight grip. To Jed's horror, Dog Jack tumbled to the ground and the two dogs locked jaws.

Jed wanted to scream, "Somebody help Jack!" but he was too frightened to say a word. His legs and arms went limp as he watched the melee. He knew he should be helping pass the buckets of water to douse the fierce fire, but was far too upset to budge from his position on the wagon.

How could he take his eyes away from the two dogs who tore into each other, ripped fur and flesh, then attacked again? Jed began to fear it was a duel to the finish – Jack's finish – but Dog Jack finally managed to back away from the savage beast. Then, with one tremendous burst of strength, he threw himself at the animal which had attacked the fire chief and sank his teeth into its throat. The shepherd yowled with pain. In vain he tried to shake Jack loose, for Jack held on with the tenacity of an octopus.

At last the Firehouse canine dropped off onto the ground, but in no way did he show a sign of defeat. Back arched, teeth bared, he snarled to warn the shepherd he was still willing to fight.

Instead of renewing the attack, the huge dog dropped his tail, gave a yelp and retreated down the street. Leaping from the wagon, Jed reached down and carefully lifted Dog Jack into his arms. Battered, wounded and exhausted from the conflict, Jed's animal friend collapsed.

Fearing the worst, Jed watched apprehensively, then breathed a sigh of relief as Jack momentarily opened his eyes. Jed pulled the dog and himself up onto the fire wagon and dabbed at Jack's many wounds with his shirt tail.

Glancing about, he was horrified to see that during the ferocious battle the fire had taken its toll. The grand old Malloy homestead was no more – the rambling house was nothing but a mass of smoldering wood.

Dejected, Matt walked slump-shouldered over to the wagon and began to load the empty buckets. Pulling himself up into the driver's seat, he took up the reins. Smudged, dirty, his shoulders sagging so that Jed knew he was bone weary, Matt sighed, "Well, we lost that one."

"Not Jack, suh. He won," Jed answered.

"I'm glad." The two friends rode back to the firehouse in silence, Matt stopping the wagon periodically to drop the volunteer firemen off near their homes.

Jed finally broke the silence. "Ya dis'pointed in me, Mistah Matt? Fizzled out at mah first fire, huh?"

Matt shrugged his shoulders. "In a way, boy. You're gonna have to learn that people are more important than animals – no matter how much you care about them. The Malloys are going to have a tough time getting a new house and belongings. They just lost everything they had in this world."

"I's sorry, Mistah Matt," Jed apologized. His head drooped in shame.

"Skip it, boy," Matt answered, dismissing the subject. "We've got something else we've got to talk over."

"What's that?"

"We voted last night at the meeting to sign up as a unit and call ourselves the Pittsburgh Volunteers. You want to go?"

Jed studied his friend. Aha! At last he understood why he had been barred from the meeting the night before. The fireman had been hashing over whether or not to go to war!

"Ya takin' Jack, suh?" Jed asked, reaching over to give Jack a light pat on the head. Matt gave Jed a half smile, then broke into a full grin. "Who'd save my life if we didn't? We couldn't leave the North's best doggone fighter at home, could we? Besides, every company needs a mascot and a boy to take care of it. That's the way I see it, don't you?"

Jed grinned in return, "Yessuh, Mistah Matt, I sho' do!"

Rank brings responsibility.

Chapter 9
Army of the Potomac

The next few days were hectic for Jed and all the men at the fire station as they readied themselves to become part of the Hundred and Second Regiment of the Pennsylvania Volunteers, also known as the Old 13th Washington Infantry. The oldest Malloy boy, Jimmy, the one who had reported the fire at his home, was recruited to be their drummer boy.

Jed would never forget the day he stood before the enlistment officer, signing up to go to war. The officer looked up and stared in unbelief as Jed approached his desk. Jed's left foot shuffled uneasily, yet the man's penetrating look never wavered.

"Name?"

"Jed, suh," Jed answered, his voice quivering along with his heart.

"SUH?" the man asked in a tone of disgust. "Now, tell me – is that your last name?"

"No, suh, jes' Jed. Nevah did have a las' name. If I did, nevah knowed what it was."

The officer leaned forward and glared at him. "What's your age, then?"

"Think I wus fo'teen in April, suh."

"Do you know anything for certain about yourself?" Sarcasm fairly oozed from his voice. "You must know there's a war and you want to join it – or do you think you're signing up to play a game of pretend?"

When the man stopped speaking he glared at Jed again. Once more Jed shuffled his foot. How he wished he could get rid of that nervous habit which involuntarily gave him away every time he was ill at ease.

"You sure you're man enough to take this man's war?"

Embarrassed, Jed hung his head. "Hope so, suh."

"And that," the man said indicating Jack's presence, "Is that your animal?"

"Yessuh. That's Dog Jack."

"It figures," the officer sneered. "He looks as intelligent as you. Here's your papers." As Jed walked away the man added curtly, "I hope you know what you're doing, but I doubt it."

Matt, who was waiting for him in the doorway demanded, "Let me see those papers, boy." Jed handed them to Matt. As he read them over his face flushed bright red.

"I knew it! – That CURR!" Matt snarled and spat on the ground.

George Brown walked over to him and asked, "What's the matter, Matt? Something sure got under your skin!"

"That character put SUH down as Jed's last name!" Matt declared in disgust. "He did everything but spit on him and Jack. I'd like to tie into him and flatten that buzzard out on the floor!"

Upset and puzzled, Jed turned to George and asked him, "Don't reckon I unnerstand, suh, why any No'thern officer treat me like that? I's signin' up to help his army."

"Officer, ha!" Matt smirked. "He's a stupid little recruiting sergeant who likes to sound big. If you let the likes of him bother you, son, you have to be crazy!"

George gave Jed a consoling pat on the back. "He's right, Jed. Not all Northerners are sympathetic to slaves. He's probably enlisting men just because it's a paying job."

"Yea," Matt scoffed, "and he won't ever have to fight like we will. He can sit on his backside in safety and fill out papers for the rest of the war."

"– And make fun of dogs," Jed mused.

The following day an official-looking envelope came through the mail. Everyone stood by as Matt opened it and read its contents. "Says here that the One Hundred and Second Regiment of the Pennsylvania Volunteers is to start for Washington, D.C., within the next two days. We're to board the train at the government's expense."

After hearing their orders the men scurried about, packing their belongings and tying up all loose ends. Most of them hurried home to prepare their families for the separation. Somehow they all managed to get ready on time.

As Jed peered into the faces of the men as they gathered at the railroad station, he detected many mixed emotions among the volunteers from the Niagara Fire Company — some anxious and willing, others more thoughtful and contemplative. He realized, as he knew they did, that they might have to fight battles which could have far greater consequences than all of the fires they had ever fought.

Dog Jack stood at the front of the line like a proud soldier. Jimmy Malloy, standing tall and erect, carried his drum over and stood beside Jack. Jed wondered how this very young lad was going to react to their departure. He wondered, too, how he himself would feel if he were leaving his family for the first time — especially going off to a war, the realities of which were still incomprehensible to him.

When Jed turned to comment to Matt, he found his friend was no longer beside him. Scanning the crowd, his eyes came to rest upon Matt's back as he leaned down talking earnestly to Molly.

When he lifted his head and turned, a softness about the way Matt was looking at his short, round wife saddened Jed. As much as Matt always complained about his spouse, Jed could see now that it was just his way, for as the train whistle gave its first shrill blast, Matt reached down and scooped his Molly up into his arms. Jed knew she must be crying, for her squat little body was heaving up and down.

Embarrassed, Jed looked away. Everywhere he turned men were embracing their wives and children. Mrs. Malloy was sobbing uncontrollably. Her husband reached out a sympathetic arm in a futile attempt to console her about her young son going off to war. Jimmy Malloy stared down at his drum, his gaze never wavering as he began to beat out a march while the others boarded the train. Even as his mother stretched out her arms toward him – her face contorted with despair – he managed to keep a stern impassive look on his young face.

Suddenly Jed felt so very alone. Everyone had someone who cared that they were leaving – someone there to see them off – everyone but himself. He wondered if he had ever felt more homesick than at that moment.

A whimper caused him to glance down at his feet. Jack's head was cocked sideways as he looked up at Jed with expectancy. Upon lifting the dog up in his arms, the warm, soft canine body created the security he had wished for – as though he, too, belonged to someone.

"Jack, boy," he whispered, "I couldn't git along without ya!"

When they boarded the train, the Niagara Volunteers all jammed into one passenger car and settled back for the long ride. As the wheels began their methodical rhythm toward Washington, Jed sat in a seat near the window so he could watch the view. Dog Jack perched high on his lap and peered out the window too. They passed a continuous panorama of Pennsylvania farms – cows, big red and white barns, horses and farmers harvesting their crops.

Finally bored with the sameness of the picturesque landscape before him, Jed returned his attention to the men in the coach. Matt slid into the seat beside him and sighed. "Well, here we are, fella. We're on our way."

"Cain't hardly believe it – can you?" Jed responded.

"And here I am," Matt said in an exasperated tone, "going to be a papa for the first time and havin' to leave my wife and unborn baby behind."

Jed gasped. "Ya gots ta be kiddin', Mistah Matt! Ain't ya excited?" It wasn't at all Matt's nature to take such a great happening with only a grain of enthusiasm. Usually he would react to such news with the zeal of a sailor on his first shore leave in five years.

Matt shrugged. "I don't know, Jed," he stated flatly. "Normally I'd be silly as a laughing hyena, but things are different now. I might never get to see my own child."

George Brown leaned back over the seat. "What's that you said, Matthew?" he asked. "I couldn't help but overhearing. – Hey, men, we have an expectant papa here with us!"

Jolly Harry Svetland, seated across from George, promptly rose to his feet and to the occasion and cried, "Hear ye, hear ye," lifting up his arms as if giving a toast. "Three cheers for Father Matthew!"

As cheers of celebration rose from the men, Jack, not to be left out of the festivities, joined in with a trio of yips. Matt's news turned the rest of the trip into bedlam. As the men teased and tormented him Jed was aware that Matt was truly enjoying every second of it, even though his face flamed often and he gruffly dismissed their wisecracks.

At last the men tired of their pastime and began to sing the words to "JOHN BROWN'S BODY." By then Matt was wound up to such a degree that he took out a scrap of paper, scribbled something on it, stretched out on the floor and put the paper across his chest. He closed his eyes and solemnly folded his hands in front of him.

The coach went into an uproar. Jed was sure their laughter could be heard clear back in Pittsburgh, but had no way of knowing what Matt's printing said. Once more he desperately wished that he could read.

When Matt finally pulled himself up off the floor, he returned to his seat beside Jed. Pointing to the sign, Jed asked him, "Mistah Matt, what dat paper say?"

Matt gaped at him for an instant, then said to him, "You're kidding, Jed. Boy, are you gonna have to learn to read! It says JOHN BROWN'S BODY!"

Belatedly, Jed laughed.

After they calmed down a bit, the men in the coach bedded down for the night. The next morning they awoke to find themselves close to Washington. There was none of the hilarity of the night before, for everyone was busy getting his belongings ready to unload.

When the train came to an abrupt stop, the men regained their balance and climbed down the steps to face the city Jed had heard so much about. So this was the nation's capital!

Jack snuggled close in his arms until an officer strode over and cried out, "Attention!" Hastily Jed put Dog Jack down on the ground, then snapped to attention with the other men. There was something about this man that commanded respect.

"I'm Colonel Rowley," the officer stated. "Welcome to Washington. You will be part of the Army of the Potomac under General McClellan. This is not a pleasure trip, men. We don't mean for you to enjoy your stay here. You're going to have to dig in and work hard if we're going to make soldiers out of you. Your barracks are in that building over to the right."

The colonel tilted his head, indicating a distinguished looking bearded man walking over toward him. "And this is Reverend A.M. Stewart," he announced in the way of introduction. "He's the chaplain of the Hundred and Second. Reverend Stewart...."

The man introduced as Reverend Stewart removed his hat, uncovering a receding hair line accentuated by a mass of bushy black hair toward the back of his head. When he opened his mouth to speak, the softness of his voice amazed Jed. "I'm pleased to meet all of you," the chaplain said, stroking his beard. "These are not easy times and it is my fervent prayer that each of you will seek me out if you need help of any kind. I do not in any way believe that I can answer all your problems, but I will take them to our Lord who certainly can – and will."

"Thank you, Chaplain," Colonel Rowley said, then curtly addressed the assembled men, "Dismissed!"

Jed turned to Matt. "Guess we's s'posed ta go to our barracks."

"Guess so. That Rowley character doesn't say any more'n he has to, does he?" Matt commented.

As they walked toward the tents which were to be their temporary dwelling places, they passed by two rather elegantly dressed young girls. Matt gave out two loud coughs, his way of informing them he was aware of their presence.

"Ya be a married man, Mistah Matt!" Jed protested in alarm.

"Know that, boy, but it doesn't hurt to look."

They were choosing their bunks when Reverend Stewart entered the barracks and approached Jed and the regiment mascot. Reaching down, he gave Dog Jack a friendly pat on the head. "Your dog, son?" he asked.

"Not really, suh." He was feeling a little uneasy as he always had with white strangers. "Jack's the company mascot. Reckon he belongs ta all of us."

When Reverend Stewart smiled, his eyes crinkled at the corners. Jed detected an extraordinary warmth in this man, a special quality which he'd seen in few men.

The chaplain extended his hand to Jed. "I think you'd have a hard time convincing this dog that you're not his master, son. He follows you around like a shadow! I guess you must know I'm Chaplain Stewart, but I must confess I can't say who you and your friend are."

The amusement that glistened in the chaplain's eyes puzzled Jed. Clasping the kind soft-spoken man's hand, he announced proudly, "I's Jed, suh. This heah's Dog Jack."

With unexpected respect, Reverend Stewart looked Jed squarely in the eye. "I know you and I'll be good friends. I plan to have a Bible study early each morning and I hope you'll attend. You can bring your canine friend, too – or doesn't he read very well?"

Jed's left foot began to shuffle. His head dropped. To his surprise he felt close to tears. "I cain't come either, Chaplain." In fact," he confessed, "..cain't read at all."

He waited for a startled reaction from Reverend Stewart, but received none. Instead he told Jed,"I knew I could do some good for somebody while I was here. Jed, how about letting me have the privilege of opening up a whole new world for you – the wonderful world of the printed page? Would you agree to spend an hour with me after supper every day?"

"Yessuh!" Jed replied eagerly.

As Reverend Stewart moved away to talk with some of the other men, Jed lifted his canine friend up near his face and spoke. "Ya know, Jack, I's confused. Chaplain's the onliest man I ever met who acted like ya was doin' him a favor while he's really doin' you one. Reckon any man be that kind?"

In the months following Jed spent much time with Chaplain Stewart and often wondered when the Presbyterian minister slept, for he not only read his Bible in his bunk until late at night, but rose early each morning to pray.

Matt had his own version of the chaplain. "I never saw such an early bird!" he told his buddies. "It's no wonder his parents gave him the initials A.M.!"

Every night Jed and Dog Jack wandered over to the chaplain's bunk for Jed's reading lesson. Reverend Stewart demonstrated such patience that Jed responded with eagerness to his willing teacher. Within a month, he had gone through his first primer.

Reverend Stewart encouraged him. "You're such a good student, Jed. I think we need to give you some writing lessons now. Would you like that?" Jed was thrilled with the prospect of learning to write under the chaplain's direction.

Much as they had at home, the men filled their evenings with cribbage and domino games interspersed with war talk. Jed enjoyed watching them play with Jack on their off hours, except for the times Jimmy Malloy spent romping with HIS dog.

Whenever Chaplain Stewart helped Jed with his lessons, the Malloy boy coaxed Jack off to play. Jed never said anything, but felt resentment building up. One night Reverend Stewart observed, "Jed, you really resent that boy playing with Jack, don't you?"

Sitting on the edge of the chaplain's bunk, Jed shuffled his foot. Shame surged through him — as though he'd been caught red-handed stealing chickens from a chicken coop.

"Guess ah do a little bit, suh," he admitted.

Stroking his dark heavy beard, Reverend Stewart stared at Jed with his gray-green eyes. "A LITTLE bit?"

Jed felt uneasy. "N-no, suh. Reckon a lot."

Chaplain Stewart spoke softly, "Admitting a problem to yourself is often half the battle of overcoming it. The other half is getting over it. The Bible says, 'Thou shalt not covet' and I'm sure that includes coveting the time others spend with your dog."

How he wished the chaplain hadn't been able to see right through him!

"He's really not mine, like I told ya, suh. He belongs ta the whole comp'ny."

The chaplain broke into one of his rare broad grins. "I doubt that Jack or you really believe that, but just the same, I'd like you to do something for me. The next time you feel bitter toward the Malloy boy, think about how homesick he must be. He's used to having brothers and sisters around to play and argue with. If you remember that, I'm sure you won't mind his playing with Jack half as much."

Jed hadn't considered Jimmy's needs. "Yessuh," he promised with appreciation as he watched the red-haired lad romp with Dog Jack. "I'll try."

That night Matt teased him about spending so much time talking with the chaplain, but Jed had noticed Matt himself often made his way over to the preacher's bunk. Every time he received a letter from Molly, Matt talked over its contents with Reverend Stewart. The baby was supposed to arrive near Valentine's Day, but that red letter day on the calendar came and went. Still there was no news from Molly. Matt was beside himself.

Chaplain Stewart tried his best to soothe the prospective papa's nerves. "Babies often arrive late, Matt. Don't fret so much." He might as well have told the sun to quit rising in the morning for all the more those words of consolation impacted Matt's fretting. He continued to fuss and fume, "I feel so helpless! There's nothing I can do!"

"Yes there is, Matt. You can pray about it."

Matt shook his head in frustration. "I mean DO something, sir – besides sit here!"

The chaplain patted the big fire chief's shoulder as he did with all the other men when he tried to encourage them. "I don't know what you think you could do at home either. Mother Nature does things in her time. Now don't worry, Matt. Put it in the Lord's hands."

Jed didn't know if Matt really prayed about it or not, but if he did, he certainly hadn't totally "put it in the Lord's hands." Each day Matt grew more restless and difficult to live with.

George Brown told him one day, "You do more barking than Dog Jack."

But Matt continued on his restless road and, finally, when on the twenty-fourth of March he received a letter, Jed felt certain it HAD to be THE ONE.

"Hurry – hurry up and open it!" Jed urged.

Nervously Matt tore open the envelope and read aloud, "Molly gave birth to a baby girl today. Both are fine. Busy now. Will write details later. Love, Mother."

"YOW-EEE!" Matt cried. "I'm a father ! I'm a FATHER!"

There was no containing him after that news. Jubilant all that day – passing out cigars he'd bought from the sutler and clapping everyone on the back excitedly he continually proclaimed, "I'M A FATHER! I'M A FATHER!"

Everyone secretly chuckled about Matt's enthusiasm – he was unable to answer their questions about the baby's birth date or her weight or any other particulars. He and Molly hadn't even agreed on a girl's name, but obviously he didn't care. He was a father!

When his next letter from Molly arrived, Matt sat on his bunk digesting it over and over. At last he glanced up and told Jed, "Boy, Molly says we're going to call her Rebecca after the Bible lady. I think it's a big name for a little baby, but I'll bet Reverend Stewart will be pleased."

Matt arose and walked over to the chaplain. Jed watched the chaplain's face light up as he heard the news, then grinned and said to Dog Jack, "I bet the preacher thinks the name's jes' fine."

Matt's joyous news was welcome among the men of Company F, for rumors around the camp indicated the whole Army of the Potomac would soon be moving out of their winter quarters for a spring offensive.

During that winter at Washington Jed felt almost detached from the war. Even though he daily marched and drilled with the troops, he witnessed no visual evidence of the horror of battle, except for the times when he caught glimpses of wounded soldiers being carried on litters into the hospitals. Jed chose to turn his back on those agonizing scenes, trying to ignore the anguished faces of the suffering men and the stench of blood which tainted the air. He refused to take in the dismal sights and sounds – soldiers crying in despair at the loss of arms, legs, hands, feet. Some bore grotesque scars, some had no limbs at all. How difficult it was to grasp the fact that he and his friends in the Niagara Volunteers could return to Washington in that same condition.

Jed was not unsympathetic, his mind simply could not take in such horror. Many of the veterans recounted their tales of battle to him and his companions and with Reverend Stewart's help he read the newspaper accounts of the war. Still Jed could not truly comprehend how sordid actual combat could be.

Their living quarters became a sanctuary for him. As he sat alone on his bunk and held Dog Jack close, the war was as unreal to Jed as a character from one of Aesop's Fables which Chaplain Stewart had been teaching him to read.

Chapter 10
The Confrontation

The Hundred and Second's A and D Companies had been dispatched to Great Falls, Maryland, to guard the Chesapeake and Ohio Canal, but Jed's Company F remained in Washington. While there Jed continued to fill his idle time by playing with Dog Jack and taking reading lessons every night from Chaplain Stewart. For him, the war still seemed very remote and far away until one day during their drill session when Colonel Rowley appeared to address the entire regiment.

"All right, men, tomorrow we move out – ALL of us. Return to quarters now and pack your gear. Get to bed early – we leave at six a.m. sharp!"

Jed felt as though he'd suddenly been drenched with a bucket full of cold water. The colonel's few sharp words had brought Mr. Lincoln's war home to him. How could he continue to feel disassociated when he was going to be a part of all the frightening war stories he had heard about?

Returning from drill session to the barracks, he pulled out his knapsack and began methodically to pack his belongings. Glancing around at the faces of Matt, Chaplain Stewart, George, Tom Drysdale, Harry Svetland and the others, he realized that each of the men was suffering similar shock. Even the chaplain's countenance revealed traces of grave concern.

Trying to appear nonchalant and unconcerned, Jed

sauntered over to Chaplain Stewart's bunk, but the chaplain's first comment made Jed aware that he could not deceive this remarkably perceptive man.

Reverend Stewart never stopped packing, never raised his head, as he asked, "Scared, boy?"

Jed's eyes opened wide in surprise. "Yessuh, how'd ya know?"

Rev. Stewart straightened up and looked squarely at him. A half smile crossed his face. "Because I am too, Jed. We all are. Don't worry though, son, we're taking along with us the Best Companion a man can have. God'll be with us every step of the way. I have His assurance."

Jed wasn't sure what the chaplain meant, but if the Reverend Stewart felt reassured, then he did too.

They bedded down early as they had been ordered, but from the rustling sounds in all the bunks Jed knew everyone shared his apprehension about the coming day. Dog Jack must have sensed the uneasiness, too, for he was as restless as the men. Jack customarily bedded himself down at the foot of Jed's bunk, but during that night Jed was roused by a canine whimper coming from the direction of Matt's cot.

"It's all right, boy," Matt whispered to comfort the dog. "We'll be all right. Now go to sleep."

Seconds later Jed felt the impact of Jack's body as the dog leaped up on his cot. Pulling Dog Jack toward him, he positioned himself so Jack could nestle in his arms. Secure with the warmth of having something alive to hold close and love — and feeling loved in return — Jed's eyelids finally gave way to sleep. At four a.m. everyone was up and on the move. As he watched the grim faces of his friends, Jed knew he had correctly interpreted the night-long rustling — he wasn't the only one who hadn't slept well. Silence reigned except for Matt's far-too-boisterous comments. He seemed to be the self-appointed committee of one in charge of bolstering everyone's morale. Because Jed knew Matt so well, he realized all the fire chief's brazen talk was primarily an effort to calm his own inner turmoil. The others must have understood, too, for no one paid any attention.

Matt reached toward the window near his bunk, lifted a curtain and peered out into the darkness. "Look, buddies," he quipped, "the dawn hasn't even found a crack to come through yet."

Since there was no reaction forthcoming from the men, Matt glanced around and asked, "Don't you get it – the crack of dawn?"

Still no one laughed or smiled, but continued with their own tasks. Finally Matt shrugged his shoulders and kept quiet, too. Jed knew from this reaction that his friend needed to talk, but none of the rest – including himself – felt up to bantering word puns back and forth with Matt.

Jed was pleased, though, when he saw Matt sit down on his bunk and lift Jack onto his lap. As the fire chief's large fingers stroked the short, bristly fur, Jed sensed that Dog Jack's presence was also consolation for Matt.

The bugle sounded at four thirty while it was still pitch black outside and the men hustled to finish their last-minute preparations. At five forty-five a.m. all the troops began to stream out into the streets. While Jed watched Chaplain Stewart and the officers mount their horses, he thought if he hadn't known better, they could have been a part of a huge Independence Day parade – the kind he and Matt and Dog Jack had gone into downtown Pittsburgh to see on the previous fourth of July.

That day, though, was not an Independence Day. It was March twenty-sixth, 1862, and Jed did not feel independent in any way. In fact, he hadn't felt more trapped in years.

Colonel Rowley rode before the troops on his elegant chestnut mare and all the soldiers snapped to attention. "All right, men, we've got a job to do and we're ready. We're to go to Alexandria and then move on with the brigade. We'll get further orders when we arrive there."

As Jed, Dog Jack, and all the men of the Hundred and Second began their march toward the long awaited first confrontation with the Rebels, Jed wished he could climb into the minds of the others to see if they shared the terror which tore at his insides. As they stepped in unison, many joined together to sing a spirited march, for they had been waiting eagerly to get personally involved in the war and envisioned themselves as potential heroes.

"We are coming, Father Abraham, 300,000 more,
From the Mississippi's winding stream and from New England's shore.
We leave our ploughs and workshops, our wives and children dear,
With hearts too full for utterance, without a single tear.
We dare not look behind us, but steadfastly before;
We are coming, Father Abraham, 300,000 more."

When they reached Alexandria, a messenger on horseback waited for them alongside the road. Colonel Rowley received the telegram offered him by the messenger from the Signal Corps. After tearing it open and scanning its contents, he turned to the waiting troops and announced, "The enemy has retreated up the peninsula. We are to pursue them all the way."

At Rowley's command, "Forward, March!" the Hundred and Second moved out again. For days and weeks they marched without even a sign of the enemy. Jed began to believe they were going to do nothing but march forever.

When the men broke rank to go off on a side jaunt along the route, Tom played his harmonica while the others sang.

By Monday, May fifth, they had become part of the Army of the Potomac, making their way into Williamsburg, Virginia. Jed turned to Matt as they marched in a downpour of rain. "Don' know, Mistah Matt. Looks like we's gonna march our way right through this war. Look at Jack! He even looks calm an' collected now."

Matt shook his head in disagreement. "Don't be so sure of yourself, Jed, I think we're in for it soon."

Before Matt could say anything more, there was a flurry of activity in the road ahead. Several soldiers in gray uniforms scurried into the fields.

"Matt!" Jed cried with horror. "They's Rebs! They's Johnny Rebs!"

Seconds later – BOOM! – the sound of an explosion filled the air. Captain McIlwaine's horse reared high and the captain sailed off his mount into a ditch at the side of the road, fanning the air with his arms and legs all the way.

"Mistah Matt," Jed cried, his eyes wide with terror, "wha' happened ta the captain? What caused that? Tweren't nobody 'round!"

"I don't know, Jed. I just don't know."

Some of the men ran to help the captain but Colonel Rowley ordered curtly, "Fall in! Leave him to the hospital corps! – And watch where you're walking. They've planted mines under the road!"

Mines? Underground? Did he mean they could be marching on top of something that could blow them to pieces? Jed cringed and intently examined the mud as he moved forward. "It's bad enough to have a enemy ya can see, Mistah Matt, but this hidden stuff shonuff spooks me! Who ever heared of 'splosives hid under the ground!"

"Look – look over there, Jed," Matt rasped, indicating gray uniformed soldiers streaming toward them off their left flank. "We must be in for quite a battle!"

Just then Chaplain Stewart, who had rushed to the aid of the wounded captain, caught up with them.

"Chaplain," Matt queried, "who's that over there?" With his hand he waved toward a group of men off to the right.

The chaplain strained to see the troops better. "Must be the Ninety-Third. I heard they were to reinforce us."

Booms sounding like thunderclaps rumbled from the outskirts of town. Although they'd been drenched by the steady downpour for some time, Jed knew immediately that the noise he'd heard was not from the rainstorm.

"Take cover!" someone yelled and blue uniforms flew in

every direction.

As soon as Jed made contact with the damp earth, he felt Dog Jack's body beside him.

"Hang on, Jack boy. We's in for it!" he cried.

"You hang on, too, Jed," a voice Jed recognized echoed. The chaplain lay just inches away from him.

A blood-curdling sound of the Rebel's battle cry, "KI-YI, KI- YI!" vibrated through the air. Jed thought a thousand Cherokees must be on the war path. Jack moved his body even closer to Jed's. "Wha's dat?" the firehouse stable boy whispered hoarsely to the chaplain.

"It's the Reb's war cry," he answered.

"What a scarey sound!" Jed whispered back emphatically.

Enemy artillery fire began to pour toward them with full force. Fourth of July fireworks in Pittsburgh were nothing in comparison. Momentarily Jed wondered why the North's cannons weren't retaliating, but then realized the South had caught them off guard! Gray coats streamed at them from all directions. One Confederate soldier stood over them, just about to pounce on their position, when a cannon from the Ninety-Third made short work of him. The mutilated body fell close to Jed and he saw at close range the agony on the dying man's face.

How could Jed find any hatred inside himself for a mortally wounded stranger even though he wore the uniform of the enemy? A squeamish, ugly twist gnarled his guts. He had watched a man die! Beside him, Dog Jack whimpered as though he, too, was flabbergasted at the goings on.

Glancing up Jed saw another gray uniform approach, this one swooping down on Matt's position. Panic struck. Without a moment's hesitancy, he raised his rifle, took aim and shot. The soldier crumbled and fell to the ground with a dreadful thud. It occurred to him what he had done.

"Oh, dear God!" he wailed, horrified. "I's killed 'im!"

Chaplain Stewart's soothing voice assured him, "If you hadn't, son, he'd have killed Matt."

Dog Jack lay motionless on the ground with Jed right beside him, his legs feeling so heavy it seemed they were shackled. He could not move, but only lie there and stare with disbelief at the slaughter taking place around him. Could there really be any sanity in what was happening? He wished he could faint to escape, but to his disappointment he did not.

Hand-to-hand combat was taking place all over the battlefield. Artillery continuously blazed hot fire back and forth between the lines; muskets were raised and bayonets fixed. The battlefield was covered with small puddles of blood and the continued fighting seemed endless. Jed felt an urge to scream and run away from the nightmare.

The men of the Hundred and Second never moved to retreat, but held their ground, continuing to send volleys of bullets toward the attacking Rebels, having no time to do anything but reload and fire their rifles time after time.

The wet, dismal day gave way to a wet, dismal night. At last the sounds of battle ceased. Jed breathed more easily and raised up to look around.

As he glanced behind him, he saw Chaplain Stewart extending a hand. "Come on, son," he said. "It's all over – for now anyway. Maybe we'll get accustomed to it someday."

Jed shook his head in disagreement. "I hopes not, suh. I shuh hopes not." He reached up, took the chaplain's outstretched hand and tugged to pull himself to a standing position.

A sergeant who Jed knew to be an army veteran from the Mexican War approached them and asked, "How're things over here, Chaplain?"

"We seem to have come out all right," Reverend Stewart responded, then asked, "How bad is the count?"

"Three dead and thirty-eight wounded," the sergeant stated as though he was reading statistics from a newspaper. Jed shuddered while the sergeant continued in a nonchalant manner, "The enemy seems to have taken a far greater loss and they can't afford it as much as we can."

The face of the dying soldier all too vivid in his memory, Jed stared at the man in dismay. He had heard firemen get far more upset over a cribbage score! Didn't anyone care if those "bodies" were men – fathers and husbands and sons who had loved ones waiting for them at home?

Jed expected the chaplain to admonish the man, but he did not. Instead he asked, "Why can't they afford the loss, sergeant? I understand there could be as many as fifty thousand Confederate troops here on the peninsula."

A sheepish smile spread across the sergeant's face as he explained, "That's what Magruder wanted us to think. They don't call him PRINCE JOHN for nothing – that old fox had no more than fifteen thousand men scurrying back and forth to fool us into thinking he had three times that many. And we fell for it! They fooled us with their QUAKER GUNS, too!"

Reverend Stewart looked puzzled. "Quaker GUNS? What are they?"

"Ha!" the sergeant snorted. "Thought a man of the cloth would know about something like that!"

"No," Reverend Stewart admitted. "I've never heard of them."

"Well, Chaplain," the sergeant said in a knowing tone of voice, "we might outnumber the enemy, but they've got some pretty crafty boys working for them. They peeled the bark off logs and painted them black. Then they rigged them up to look like cannons – that's what they call QUAKER GUNS. They've learned some other tricks, too, and you've already seen how effective their land mines are. I guess they've buried them all over – a sneaky, low-down trick, but they don't seem to have any consciences."

Stopping just long enough to get his second wind, the sergeant continued, "One of the men from the Ninety-Third told me about the observation balloon we had anchored to the banks of the Potomac. Seems as though General Fitz John was in it when a strong wind broke it loose from its mooring and it drifted down past the Confederate lines. I guess every trigger-happy Southerner for miles around took a pot shot at it before a change in the wind blew our old runaway gas bag back North. Now, if you've ever met old Fitz John, you'd appreciate it more – he's one of those bouncy, energetic know-it-alls. The thought of him flying around in an observation balloon half scared to death is more hilarious than I can stand." He howled with laughter.

As the sergeant walked away, the ambulance men continued to carry wounded soldiers – litter after litter – from the battlefield. Perplexed, Jed turned to the chaplain and commented, "Talk 'bout a runaway gas bag! I's sorry, suh, I jes' don' unnerstand. We jes' finished our fuhst battle. Men's hurtin; and dyin' all over this battlefield. An' he stands there thinkin' somethin's funny!"

Rev. Stewart reached over and touched Jed's arm lightly. "I know, son, but don't judge him too harshly. He's a professional soldier and a veteran of many campaigns – he can't take each man's injuries too much to heart. If he did, he'd lose his mind. You'll have to excuse me now, Jed, or I'm going to lose my job. I just came over to make sure you were all right, then got detained when I met up with him."

The chaplain started to walk away, but turned again toward Jed. "Try not to dwell too much on what happened, son. Tomorrow is another day."

Dog Jack, who lay at Jed's feet, looked up and whimpered sorrowfully, as if he, too, were trying to understand what had taken place. Jed reached down and tenderly lifted him up in his arms. Together they surveyed the results of their first day in combat. Jed spoke woefully to his companion, "Don' know, Jack friend, if we be wantin' tomorrow ta come or not."

Artillery.

Chapter 11
Conflict at Savage Station

Once initiated into warfare, the Hundred and Second Regiment was involved in one skirmish or battle after another. During those clashes, Dog Jack swiftly learned the basic skills of a true soldier and soon put aside any sense of cowardice. Dodging musket fire, bayonets and cannon shells, he ran through the battlefields carrying water to the wounded. Jed, influenced by Jack's bravado, became more courageous as he watched his dog maneuver back and forth administering help to the men. In no way did this fearless animal resemble the wobbly, uncertain stray that had found its way to the fire station.

Dog Jack also learned to respond to the sounds of the bugle, reacting immediately and accurately to the calls to attack or retreat. Jed never ceased to be amazed at the intelligence of his canine friend. Dog Jack demonstrated true allegiance to the members of the Pittsburgh Volunteers. Whenever one of their men was hit by a bullet or struck by a sword, Jack rushed quickly to his side.

In the heat of one battle, Jed helplessly watched as Tom Drysdale crumpled. Immediately Jack ran to his side. Jed was relieved when Tom sat up and stroked the dog. He'd obviously been only stunned.

Nearing the end of June, after several days of fierce opposition, they were forced to take up a defensive position at a place called Savage Station. Suddenly the crack of gun fire and the roar of exploding shells frightened Jed. The pungent smell of the sulfur smoke was so overpowering that Jed stopped to gasp for breath. Magruder's men advanced on them with heavy artillery fire until at last the bugler sounded the call to retreat.

Grateful for the bugle's message, he urged Jack, "Come on, boy, let's git out a heah!" Always reluctant to respond to the call to flee from the enemy, Dog Jack hesitated for a moment, then followed.

Jed raced through a clump of trees until he reached a small clearing. There he threw himself down. As he and Jack sprawled behind the protection of the thicket, Jack panted rapidly, trying to get his second wind. Jed sympathized. His own chest felt as though it would surely burst.

Just as he whispered to Dog Jack, "Phew! We's made it!" something hard and stiff poked against the former slave boy's back. A gruff voice growled, "That's what you think, nigger!" The hair on Jed's arms bristled. An uncontrolable cold chill surged through his entire body. Jed whirled from lying on his stomach to his back and looked straight up into the face of a Confederate soldier who was pointing his rifle down at him.

Jack must have sensed the impending danger. With a whimper he inched closer to Jed whose heart pounded faster than Jimmy Malloy's drum as he beat out a call to attack.

"March!" the soldier ordered. His crisp no-nonsense command caused Jed to automatically spring to his feet and do as he was told. Jack followed at his heels. Jed's captor pushed him along with the muzzle of his rifle. As they continued to make their way through a clump of trees, the ground beneath their feet became swampy and Jed found it increasingly difficult to walk fast enough to suit the man in gray. Every time he stopped long enough to extract one of his feet from the mire, the gruff voice would insist, "Keep moving, nigger!" He emphasized his orders by poking Jed's back over and over again with the end of his rifle.

Afraid of what his captor's next move might be, Jed managed to do as he was told. There was something indescribably authoritative and frightening about that hard piece of steel shoving against his spine. Feelings of uneasiness swept from the top of his head to the soles of his feet, for he had never been captured before. How he hoped Jack wouldn't try to attack this Johnny Reb! The muzzle of the man's rifle butt was too pressing for comfort. Jed sensed from the determined set of his jaw that the soldier would gladly shoot him for even a minor reason.

When at last they neared a clearing, a tent surrounded by gray uniformed soldiers came into view. With the end of the rifle still pressed against his ribs, Jed's captor marched him up to a table positioned directly outside the door of the tent where a Confederate sergeant was doing paper work.

"Look what I have, sir!" the soldier boasted as though he'd returned with a hunting trophy.

As the sergeant looked up from his work and saw the soldier's prize, Jed sensed more hatred in that man's eyes than he had ever seen in any other's. For a moment which seemed like an eternity, he continued to stare, then coldly and calculatingly he snarled, "If I had my way, you'd be dead, you black cur, you! Get inside!"

Jed cringed. No one, not even Kirk's father, had ever talked to him so brutally. Evidently the sergeant was so distraught at seeing a black captive that he hadn't even noticed his new prisoner's dog lying on the ground. Dog Jack followed Jed into the prison compound without the sergeant saying a word about him. This pleased the dog's master immensely. Maybe, just maybe, they'd let his dog live.

Inside the small tent a group of Union soldiers huddled together, but, as Jed scanned the many faces, he couldn't find one that looked familiar.

"Well, guess we did it, boy," Jed lamented as he sat beside the others. Dog Jack settled down in his lap while he stroked his fur. "We seem to have left all our friends behind."

Later, for lack of anything better to do, Jed walked out through an opening in the opposite side of the tent. Scanning the wire fence surrounding the area, he saw no visible means of escape at that moment. Jed squatted on the ground and watched the Confederate guards marching back and forth. He could not keep from staring at the back of the one who had just walked by a second time. What was so familiar about the soldier's stance and the shape of his head?

"No! It couldn't be," Jed mumbled under his breath. But as the soldier made an about-face and began to march back toward him once again, Jed opened his mouth in disbelieving recognition.

"Kirk!" he whispered hoarsely, rising to his feet.

The young soldier stopped short as though confronted by a ghost. To Jed's astonishment, Kirk's eyes misted as he gasped, "Jed, I thought you were dead!"

Over and over again Kirk repeated, "Jed! Jed, am I glad to see you!"

Confused, Jed declared, "I cain't unnerstan', Kirk. Thought ya'd nevah have any mo' time fo' me! Ya nevah said one word ta me after mah troubles wiff yo' father."

Kirk's eyes filled with tears, one finding its way down his cheek. Then his other eye began to overflow. "I was so afraid you'd feel that way. I watched helplessly as my father beat you and it upset me so that I vowed I'd never let anyone hurt you again – not if I could help it!"

Jed swallowed hard. He stared at the young man whose expression was so sincere he doubted he could be masking ulterior emotions. The flood of tears, the troubled look were all too real.

"Sorry, Kirk," Jed admitted. "Musta judged ya wrong."

Kirk shrugged his shoulders. "Can't blame you. But tell me, Jed, how did you ever get here?"

"That's a long story, Kirk. I runned off ta Pittsburgh an' the men there at the fire station tuck me in. When they volunteered I joined up with 'em." Reaching down, he patted his dog. "This heahs Dog Jack," he said proudly. "He's our company mascot – bes' in the Union army. Have ta tell ya all mah story some other time. Tell me now," he inquired anxiously, "how's mah family?"

Kirk's face clouded. For a moment he seemed to be searching for the proper words. "I'm sorry, Jed. I don't know how to tell you, but they're gone. They were killed in a marauder's raid which burnt the whole plantation. Everything in sight burned!"

Jed stared at his friend in an attempt to comprehend what he was hearing. "Ya mean – UNION MEN KILLED MAH FAMILY?" he asked in disbelief. "Mammy? Shadow?" He could say no more. The impact of never seeing his kinfolk again was more than he could bear.

Again tears amassed in Kirk's eyes. With difficulty he managed to add, "Yes, Jed, and my family too."

Staggered by the shocking message Kirk had relayed to him, Jed simply was unable to communicate further. He turned and walked away from Kirk. Helplessness consumed him. Sitting on the ground by the fence, legs stretched in front of him, he held Jack and brooded about the outrageous act which had taken his family away from him.

The knot in his stomach and the lump in his throat intensified as the full meaning of Kirk's words hit him. The men who did that terrible thing to his loved ones were connected with Mr. Lincoln's army! That fact was more than he could comprehend. He had always believed in his heart that all the bloodshed had been necessary – that the Union was all right and the South was all wrong. Realization brought anguish. For the first time in that civil strife he understood why the South, too, felt they had reason to engage in such bloody fighting.

Throughout the afternoon he sat immobilized by the fence, daydreaming and reliving his childhood. His mother and sister's faces kept appearing in his mind's eye as he remembered them from long ago. He'd always assumed that somehow his family would be reunited some day, that he would feel again the warmth of his mother's arms as she swooped him to her bosom and cried, "Jed, boy! Oh, Jed!"

Ever since his escape from Master Cooper's plantation

he'd spent many lonely hours visualizing that scene over and over again. Neither his mind nor his heart could accept the fact that now it never could be.

Fingering Jack's short fur, he whispered softly, "Mammy, Mammy," but the sound of the endeared nick-name he would never have need to use anymore was simply too much for him to bear. "Oh, Jack," he moaned, "wish ya'd help me unnerstand."

The more he pondered, the more he yearned for the companionship of the one man he knew would sympathize with his feelings. "Gotta find the preacher, Jack. We gotta git out o' here!" He seriously began to plot their escape from the prison compound and decided the gate was the only possible way out.

At dusk he and Jack lurked in the shadows of the tent until he thought the coast was clear. Glancing to the right and left, he was sure no one was in sight. "Come on, boy," he whispered. "Now be our chance."

With a burst of speed he ran toward the gate, but out of the corner of his eye he saw a guard charging toward them. Just as he came close enough for Jed to recognize him, the guard raised his rifle. Dog Jack bared his teeth, snarled and was ready to pounce upon the soldier when Jed exclaimed, "KIRK!" Then turning to Jack, he ordered, "Down, boy, he's a friend."

For a brief moment which seemed like an eternity he and Kirk stared at one another, each young man struggling to decide what his next move should be. Jed had never been more aware of the bond which existed between them. No political war, no civil strife could make him turn against that young man he loved almost as a brother. In that brief moment the realization hit him full force.

Kirk must have shared his feelings, for, after looking all around him, he moaned, "Why would I have to be on guard duty now?" Then he slowly dropped his rifle to his side, swung open the gate and whispered frantically, "Hurry up! Get out of here before I have to change my mind!"

Jed raced through the open gate to the edge of the

clearing where the White Oak Swamp began. He and Dog Jack stopped short and pivoted around momentarily. Kirk stood by the compound looking in their direction. Jed was grateful it was dark enough that he couldn't see the expression on his friend's face. For a second he stood, longing to go back and throw himself in Kirk's arms, for he was the one last link Jed had with his childhood. He saw Kirk wave his rifle as if to say, "Go on!"

"Let's go, Jack," Jed sighed as they began to find their way back through the marsh. It was not an easy path to follow — the gloom of the night and the burdensome news of that day made the way long and weary. As they trudged through one marsh after another, only Jack's comforting presence and thoughts of receiving the chaplain's sympathy and understanding drove Jed on.

While making their way through the wet swamp land, they reached a point where Jed was walking waste deep in muck and water. Dog Jack swam ahead of him. Suddenly Jack stopped. With lightning precision he lunged forward. A snake! Horrified, Jed drew back and watched as Jack and the snake thrashed in the water. In a matter of seconds the battle was over. Triumphantly the dog swam toward Jed with a portion of the dead snake in his jaws.

"A water moccasin!" Jed cried. "Jack, ya done saved our lives agin!"

Jed remembered Matt claiming, "Moss only grows on the north side of trees, Jed. If you're ever lost you can find your way home" — so he watched the trees carefully so as not to head south again.

Finally the great swamp oaks disappeared behind them and the two escapees reached a clearing where they stood very still, breathing in the welcome aroma of burning timber and gazing longingly at the campfires in the distance. In the twilight Jed could see the soldiers were wearing that welcome shade of blue — not gray.

"They's our men!" Jed exclaimed with ecstasy.

Dog Jack sprawled out exhausted at his feet until Jed coaxed him by saying, "Come on, come on, fella, we's 'most home!"

When they reached the campfires Jed wandered from one group to another, hunting the men of his own Company F. At last he came upon a circle of familiar faces; his eyes scanned the group until they came to rest on Matt's broad face. "Mistah Matt, wheah's the chaplain?" Jed asked anxiously.

With a broad smile, his large friend rose to his feet, obviously relieved to see him. "Jed, where've you been?" he asked.

"Tell ya later," Jed answered. "After I's talked to Chaplain Stewart. Do ya know where he is? I needs ta see 'im NOW!"

Matt looked at him curiously for a moment then pointed to the left toward a silhouette by a tree. "Over there," Matt replied.

Jed turned and tiptoed quietly up behind Rev. Stewart, his familiar kneeling position indicating he was probably in prayer and would prefer not to be disturbed.

Just as Jed arrived directly behind the chaplain he came to a startled stop, for he could not believe the preacher's words of recognition. "Glad you're back, son. I've been expecting you."

"How'd ya know who it was?" Jed asked, stymied by his friend's perception of things unseen.

Chaplain Stewart sat down on a fallen log, making sure there was room beside him. "Here, Jed, sit down and tell me what's bothering you."

Again the preacher's insight amazed Jed. He asked his perceptive friend, "How do ya know I's troubled, suh?"

The chaplain smiled warmly. "I know you quite well – don't you think?"

"Guess so, suh," Jed agreed, "but ya'd nevah b'lieve my problem now."

"Tell me," the chaplain urged and Jed began unburdening his heavy load by spilling out the sad tale of being captured and learning about the loss of his family that day. Chaplain Stewart listened attentively and without comment as Jed filled him in on all the details of his woeful story. Several times Jed's voice choked up uncontrollably from the emotional upheaval he felt inside, but when he finally finished, the chaplain reached across the log and grasped Jed's hand in his. "Jed," he said softly, "I know you would feel better if you'd only cry. The Lord gave us tears as an outlet for our emotions."

Seated on that log, with Dog Jack by his feet and the chaplain by his side, he could release no tears to help relieve the wounds which were smarting from within. They were far too numerous and too deep.

Calvary ready to charge.

Chapter 12
Journey Through the Swamp

While Jed talked to his friend the chaplain, Jack plunked down on top of Jed's weary feet and promptly began to snore. After a short while, the weight of the dog's body made Jed's feet tingle as though they too had fallen asleep. He tried to move them carefully in order to get the blood circulating again without disturbing the dog, but Jack was instantly awake and alert.

"You two look bone weary," the chaplain observed with a look of concern. Pointing to a high, dry spot just to the right of the campfire, he suggested, "You'd better take Jack over there and bunk down. You both look as though you could use a good night's sleep – maybe a week of it!"

Jed obediently followed his pastor friend's suggestion. Spreading out the only blanket in his knapsack, he leaned down, took off his shoes, then gratefully threw himself across the blanket. Dog Jack snuggled up against his chest and the two of them lay quietly, luxuriating at the chance to rest. In seconds both were asleep.

It seemed to Jed that he had hardly closed his eyes when he heard a familiar voice saying, "Wake up, boy! Wake up! We're movin' out!"

His eyelids felt weighted down. Jed fought to lift them, but it seemed he simply could not. At last he forced them open and Matt's face came into focus in the dim light from the campfire.

"Come on, come on, boy," Matt coaxed. "We're supposed to get everyone across the swamp by morning. Since we're here at the rear flank we'll be the first to move out."

Jed sat up and looked about him. Dog Jack groaned in protest of the premature awakening, but then stood upright beside Jed like any true soldier facing a conflict.

After the soldiers had doused the campfire, there was no light except for the few times the moon found a peekhole in the clouded sky, and occasionally a soldier passed by with a lit candle on the end of his bayonet.

Soon the night came alive with the sound of troops shuffling their feet across the wooden bridge and a train's wheels rhythmically clicking against the rails.

There were no loud sounds – no bugles, no train whistles, no barked commands – only the whir of muted voices and the interspersed hissing of steam escaping from the train's engines.

At the command, "Light candles," each man affixed a candle to his bayonet and struck a match to light it. Suddenly the night was illumined with hundreds of candles.

Jed and Dog Jack trudged wearily beside Chaplain Stewart who was mounted on his horse. As they made their way through the swamp, Jed felt uneasy about a massive swaying silhouette clawing at the sky, even though he knew it was nothing more than a cluster of white oak trees growing out of the marshy land. He knew the swampland better than most – only the day before he had escaped through this area known as "White Oak Swamp."

Dog Jack appeared to be lost and bewildered. Walking along beside Jed and the horse Chaplain Stewart rode, he whimpered and whined. The chaplain leaned down to Jed and said in a low voice, "Poor Jack. I think he's trying to ask what in the world are we doing in this Godforsaken marsh and why are we retreating."

As Jed tugged to extract his water-soaked shoes from a swampy pithole, he also wondered the same question. What were they doing? Where were they going?

Just before dawn the "Douse the candles" order came. The black sky faded into a deep purple and gold streaks burst forth from the horizon as night gave way to dawn. Jed was staring at this panorama in the sky when suddenly – BOOM! BOOM! BOOM! – a series of nerve-shattering explosions went off behind them.

He whirled about, seeking to discern the cause of the noise and was amazed to see wood and debris flying through the air. "The bridges!" he cried aloud. Before he had time to think further, Chaplain Stewart's horse whinnied and reared high, throwing the unsuspecting chaplain down to the ground. Seconds later, the chaplain ran after his mount with Dog Jack and Jed following.

As they chased after the horse, Jack barked continually as if to scold the alarmed runaway for leaving them behind. The thin oak limbs slapped across their faces as they pursued single file; the sodden earth weighted down their shoes, but with persistence they continued their chase until they came into a clearing. Once out of the marshy woods, the horse gained more momentum and galloped across a pasture field toward the round knob of a hill.

Jed and the chaplain stopped running and stood at the edge of the clearing for a moment to catch their breath. Dog Jack continued the chase, still barking determinedly, but even Jack's legs were no match for those of the frightened steed. At last, when he could speak without huffing and puffing, the chaplain declared, "Might as well call Jack back here. We have no way to catching that runaway horse now."

As Jed put his fingers to his mouth and gave a long shrill whistle, Jack stopped abruptly, made an about-face, then raced back toward the two men.

Jed reached down and stroked the dog, saying, "Nevah mind, boy. Nevah mind. We has ta go back – maybe we kin catch 'er later." At that moment an appalling thought crossed Jed's mind. "Reverend Stewart, suh! Yo' horse has all yo' gear packed on 'er!"

"I know, son. Even my Bible – and I can't imagine what I'll do without it. I hope you're right and we do catch up to her later!"

Jed smiled. Imagine the chaplain worrying about losing his Bible! "I wou'n't worry 'bout losin' the Good Book, suh. Ya musta memo'ized all of it in yo' heart and head by now."

The preacher nodded his head in amazement at the lad's confidence in him and the two friends and their canine companion trudged back to the line where Matt greeted them with the less-than- welcome words, "Fool horse! She got away again, didn't she?"

Jed grimaced. Certainly Matt could see the horse wasn't with them. Couldn't he understand the chaplain felt badly enough without asking such a ridiculous question?

At that moment a sergeant strode toward them. His swift determined steps indicated urgency. "Hurry, men, hurry!" he ordered in a rasp of a whisper. "The Rebs are closing in on us!"

As Jed, Matt, Jack and Chaplain Stewart fell in beside the others, Matt asked, "Did the Rebs blow the bridges, Sarge?"

A frown crossed the soldier's face. "We blew them, but it hasn't seemed to delay the enemy. They're crossing that swamp as though it were dry land. It just so happened that we hit here before the real heavy rainy season, otherwise they'd never get through without the bridges. McClellan hoped we'd get to the gunboats before the Rebs caught up with us. Since we didn't, we've been ordered to make a stand on that hill over there."

He pointed to the same knob where Jed and Chaplain Stewart had last seen the chaplain's horse. "That's Malvern Hill, according to McClellan's orders," the sergeant added.

Chapter 13
Stand-Off at Malvern Hill

Jackson refused to fight on Sunday, so the Yanks had opportunity to slip through the swamp and set up on Malvern Hill. The men hustled about the hillside, getting ready for the enemy onslaught expected the next day. As they posted their huge cannons to shower grapeshot on the enemy as the Rebs swept across the fields around the gentle slopes, Jed, Dog Jack, Matt and the chaplain hurried to the back of the knoll to search again for Reverend Stewart's horse.

"Well, I'll be!" Matt exclaimed as they spied her grazing as if it were in the middle of a peaceful pasture. "That stupid filly doesn't know the right time to be afraid. If she could see those Johnny Rebs who are chasing us, she'd turn tail and run so fast she'd be in Virginia by morning!"

After halfheartedly stroking his horse's neck, the chaplain reached up to extract his Bible from his knapsack. Quickly examining the Book, he smiled broadly. "Thank God," he exclaimed, "the lost is found!"

Jed shook his head. How could he ever be able to figure out the chaplain's feelings about that Book? From observing his actions, Jed assumed that Chaplain Stewart cared far more about his Bible than he did his horse.

With the chaplain riding his horse in the lead, the three returned to the front of the hill to take up their positions with the other Niagara Volunteers. Amused as he watched

Dog Jack follow closely on the horse's heels, Jed laughed and commented to the chaplain, "I think Jack's turnin' into a watch dog. Seems 's though he wants ta make sure yo' mount don't git away agin, suh."

Reverend Stewart nodded his head affirmatively and smiled. "I hope you're right, Jed. That mare doesn't seem to think she has to stick with me!"

The following hours were nerve-frazzling as the Volunteers stared into the face of the enemy. "Why don't they do something? – anything!" Matt asked with his usual impatience. Both sides stood in readiness, but no one made a move. Jed felt they were playing a game of cat and mouse, the South being an oversized cat about to spring on its prey.

Suddenly the sound of a rifle shot penetrated the air. The enemy had made the initial move, opening fire. After their smattering of small arms fire, the big Federal guns immediately retaliated with a mighty roar. Jed watched Confederate men falling like flies as the grape-like ammunition exploded in clusters of attacking soldiers. He was certain that winning the battle would be a cinch.

"Do ya really think, Mistah Matt, that they's gonna let us git away with no mo' of a battle than this?"

"Doubt it," Matt answered. "The Rebs don't want us to escape back to the protection of our gunboats. I heard that McClellan is back on the James River now, looking the boats over and figuring out the best positions for us."

Jed gulped. Even though McClellan was proclaimed by some as a "do nothing" soldier, his presence had always given Jed reassurance. But now, when they were faced with a possible full-scale battle, their general wasn't there.

Since there was nothing he could do about the situation, he settled back with the rest of the Union troops to tensely await the enemy's next move. Uneasiness welled up inside him. Why didn't someone do something?

At four that afternoon Jed found the answer to his question and learned the size and thrust of the enemy attack. One rifle shot was heard, then bedlam broke loose. He cringed at the happenings before his eyes. It looked as though the whole Southern army had suddenly amassed and was running toward them with bayonets fixed and rifles raised. "KI-YI-KI-YI" rose up again like a horrible savage Indian war cry as the horses, men and wagons thundered toward the hillside.

"Chaplain Stewart, why they makin' that ungodly sound?" Jed asked as his heart played leap frog inside his chest.

"Same reason as you whistle in the dark, son. They're no different than we are. They're scared to death."

Even Jack, who had become a veteran soldier, cowered down beside Jed as masses of Confederate soldiers continued to charge toward the hill. Not even the huge cannons seemed to be able to stop the onslaught. The noise, the confusion, the stench of gun powder and sulfur smoke all added to Jed's fears. How could they stop the enemy's advance toward them?

Matt moaned as he stared at the slaughter at the bottom of the hill. "Every one of Lee's men must be here!" he cried.

In horror Jed watched some of his companions — men of their own Company F — as they fell beneath the musket and artillery fire of the Southerners. With unbelief he saw his friends Jim Porter, Marcus Barker and both the O'Meally brothers lose their lives by volleys of the enemy's continual gunfire. As Jed witnessed the excessive bloodshed he thought, *Shonuff's a terrible way ta die!*

The strategic placement of the Federal guns seemed to be of little advantage, for wave after wave of Confederate troops screamed as they advanced toward the bottom of the hill.

Jed, Matt and the chaplain were situated about halfway up, but it soon became evident they were not going to be able to avoid a personal confrontation with the enemy. There seemed to be no way of stopping the gray-coated soldiers who were battling their way toward them. As one group fell beneath Yankee artillery, others approached from behind. "There's no end to them!" Matt wailed.

In an instant Jed and those nearby were no longer spectators, but participants. A few enemy men had made it past the base of the hill. Turning his head left to glance at Matt, Jed cried in alarm. A Rebel soldier stood poised to shoot directly at his friend. Before Jed could react, Dog Jack jumped up between Matt's huge frame and his enemy. The bullet intended for Matt tore into Jack's side. With a thud the dog fell to the ground. As Matt reached out in a futile attempt to comfort their mascot, a second Reb bullet ripped his own shoulder.

Disregarding any danger to himself, Jed leaped to his feet. His leg was hit in the cross fire. The pain felt like scalding hot water flowing through his leg, but Jed scrambled to grasp the rocks in order to tug and pull himself, managing to reach Dog Jack's still form and painfully arch his body over his canine friend to protect him from any further injury.

Jed had seen a lot of horror since he had joined the war, but never anything like that battle. Cannons thundered from the hillside causing the ground to quiver beneath him and Dog Jack. Jed was aware that their heavy artillery outclassed the South's. How he wished he could do something for the giant of a man from Pittsburgh who had given him a place to live, and for the dog which had endeared itself to him the moment it had eaten the prized piece of candy from his hand. Helpless, he lay still, too frightened to move.

Glancing about, he found Matt responding as he had back in Pittsburgh at the Sweeney fire – again he was ignoring the dog. Even though Jack had saved his life for a second time, Matt continued to battle the opposition as though Jack hadn't been hit.

At last the fighting ceased. An eerie silence pervaded. Litter bearers rushed around the hillside rescuing the wounded. Jed raised from his lying position, grimacing at the pain in his leg, and looked across the field and the hill which had only hours before been a placid country scene. Jed thought it resembled a giant red, gray and blue caterpillar pulsating with bleeding, agonizing men. The moans and cries of agony were almost too much for him to bear.

"Hurry up and fill that wagon with the dead," an officer commanded a burial detail. "We don't want the wounded to lose heart by seeing how many were killed."

As carefully as he could, Jed rolled off Dog Jack. The dog never stirred. Matt, holding his wounded shoulder, made his way over where they lay side by side. Reaching down with his good arm, he tenderly lifted Dog Jack. With difficulty Jed managed to stand and then limp along behind Matt as he walked down the hillside. From behind he watched Matt's huge body heave with compulsive sobs as he made his way through bodies, wounded and dead, to the hospital tent. As they passed by the remainder of Company F, others wept, too, at the sight of their brave mascot who had fallen. The unbearable knot in Jed's belly swelled uncomfortably, but still he could not cry.

When they entered the tent, a surgical assistant glanced up and asked angrily, "What're you bringing that fool dog in here for?"

"Cause he's dying and he needs help," Matt answered simply.

"Good heavens, man, so do these men!" the corpsman exclaimed.

"Yeah, but he needs help NOW!" Matt retaliated.

"So do they! After we wade through the treatment of these poor souls — if we ever do get done — we'll work on your...DOG!" the corpsman protested brusquely and walked away.

Struggling to keep his balance, since Matt only had the use of one arm and it was filled with the limp form of Dog Jack, he awkwardly sat down on the ground and placed Jack's still body across his lap. Matt's massive hand caressed the dog so tenderly that Jed, in his shattered emotional condition, could hardly watch. He plunked down beside Matt, noticing an increasing stiffness in his leg, just as the medical officer turned and said sarcastically, "We could use some help, you two. If you'd just lend your able bodies to do some of the work, we could get through faster!"

As Matt carefully placed Jack on the ground, the severity of his own wound became obvious. Blood spurted from his shoulder. Jed tried to lift himself up, but as he put his weight on the wounded leg, the pain was even more unbearable than it had been while he was sitting down. He grimaced.

The medical man stared at them open-mouthed. "Good grief! You're both wounded!" he exclaimed in surprise.

"Not THAT bad – the dog's worse!" Matt protested.

"I can't believe your concern for that stupid-looking mutt! We'll be with the THREE of you as soon as we can," the man answered sarcastically and walked away.

Jed was beginning to feel they were going to be left there to squat on that hospital tent floor forever when Reverend Stewart pulled up the flap of the tent and looked in. Seeing his friend reassured Jed that somehow things would be all right.

"Oh, there you are!" Reverend Stewart exclaimed with relief. "The battle's over. We won. I saw you carrying Jack down the hill, so I knew you were both at least able to navigate. I felt I had to minister to the dead and dying first, and I didn't think anything I could say would help Jack much. How badly is he wounded?"

"Bad," Matt answered. "It looks like a bullet went through his shoulder and his side."

"And how about you?" the chaplain inquired of him.

"Just a little hole in the shoulder. I think Jed's really in worse shape. He got it in the leg."

Because Jed had been moving his leg quite a bit, the wound was again bleeding profusely. "Let me see, Jed," the chaplain requested. Slowly and painfully Jed extended his leg toward him.

Chaplain Stewart took a handkerchief from his pocket and wrapped it tightly above the wound. Tying a knot, he twisted the cloth a bit as he said, "There, that'll keep it from bleeding so much. Untwist it once in a while to keep the blood flowing."

"Thank ya, suh." Jed wondered then as he had so often – what would he do without this remarkable man of God?

After what seemed to be an endless interim, the surgeon's assistant returned to them. "All right, you two," he said, "let's get you fixed up now."

Jed looked down at the wounded dog. The battle outside had been won, but the one inside him continued to rage. Dog Jack's body hadn't even twitched since they'd arrived at the medical tent. He doubted his Dog Jack was still alive, but hadn't found the courage to ask Matt if he could find a heartbeat. Although a burning sensation in his own leg persisted, he wanted the doctor to help Jack first.

Matt echoed his thought. "Please work on the dog NOW. We can wait."

The medical man looked inquiringly at Jed who assured him, "I feel the same way, sir."

With an impatient look of disgust, the man announced, "My job is to mend soldiers."

"He IS a soldier, sir," Matt argued, "one of the best the Union has. He's saved my life twice."

Upon hearing this fact, the man's face softened. "I've never seen two more obstinate people!" Reaching down, he lifted Jack close to his face to listen for a heartbeat. Jed felt his own heart might stop as he waited for the medical man's verdict.

The surgeon's assistant shook his head. "His pulse is so faint I doubt if he can survive surgery, but obviously there's no other way to help him."

While trying to prevent panic from taking control of his voice Jed tried to reason with the man: "But, suh, ya GOT ta TRY!"

Recognizing Jed's voice and hearing his plea, Chaplain Stewart, who was talking with one of the other wounded men, excused himself and walked over to them. The medical man turned to him and explained, "These soldiers act like they won't live if their dog doesn't. They actually want us to do surgery on this – DOG – first!"

The chaplain nodded. "I'd appreciate it, too, sir. Jack's

a real morale booster to our whole regiment."

"I'm a surgical assistant," the man retorted, then shrugged his shoulders in defeat. Without another word he carried Jack over to the screened-off area used for surgery. For Jed, until that moment the delay in helping Jack had been exasperating, but knowing the dog's life was in peril made the waiting interminable.

Relieved that his canine friend would finally be given the medical attention he needed, Matt had buried his head in his hands, closing his eyes as if in prayer. Jed leaned over to Reverend Stewart and whispered, "Chaplain, suh, reckon it's all right ta pray fer a DOG?"

Reverend Stewart reached over and patted Jed's back. "I don't know about that, son, but I DO KNOW there's no reason why you shouldn't ask a Friend to save a friend."

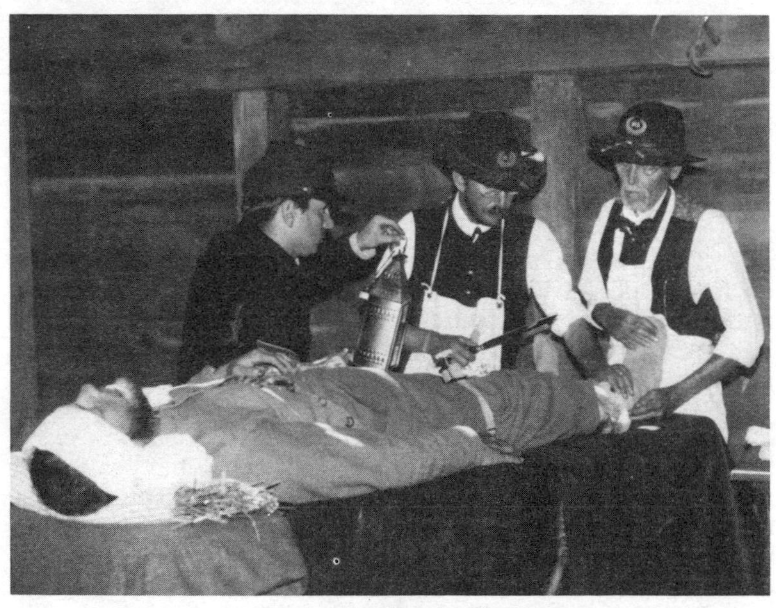

Leg amputation by surgical team.

Chapter 14
The Waiting Game

Patting Jed gently on the shoulder again, the chaplain told him, "I have to see if I can help the others, Jed, but I'll be back later to check on you and Matt." He walked away. A few feet further beyond the place where the two restlessly waited the outcome of the surgery in progress, Chaplain Stewart stopped abruptly and turned around. In a solemn tone he added, "...and on Jack too."

Minutes dragged by. Jed wished that Reverend Stewart could have stayed to watch and wait with them. Matt, his eyes closed, sat slouched down in a corner of the tent. Jed sensed from the expression on his friend's face that his shoulder hurt much more than he had let on. He wanted to talk to someone about Jack but knew Matt well enough to recognize his closed eyes and firmly clenched jaw meant, "I'm in agony, leave me alone."

Feeling anything but physically comfortable himself, Jed gently placed his hand on his burning leg, his concern for Jack's life causing a great upheaval inside him. The medical men had given him no encouragement about Jack's prospects and he wondered how he was going to cope if his faithful dog friend died.

With every passing moment Jed's fear increased. He stared at the curtained-off area. Shadows and mumbling indicated nothing definite. Jed's stomach flipped as throughout the tent moans and cries continued to come from men anguished with pain. Everywhere he looked he saw other suffering soldiers – some with missing legs and others without arms. Many had their bodies almost completely wrapped with bandages. One man wore a patch over his right eye; Jed wondered squeamishly if he had lost it. Since there was neither a whimper nor a whine from the dog Jed feared Jack had never regained consciousness.

At last the curtain lifted and the medical officer came out carrying Jack's still form, his side swathed in bandages. Jed searched the medical man's face for a hint of the verdict about Jack's possibilities, but his expression never changed from the grim, tired look he had worn when he carried the dog into the surgical area.

"Here he is, lad," the man said with surprising kindness as he placed Jack in Jed's arms. Matt opened his eyes and searched the face of the corpsman, then asked the question Jed had been afraid to put into words, "Is he going to make it, sir?"

The surgeon's assistant answered with indecisive hesitance. "I-I don't know. ...He's in shock – lost an awful lot of blood...but I managed to get the bullets out and clean around the wound. Now whether or not he lives or dies depends on how strong and determined he is."

For the first time Jed felt a sense of relief. Fingering the massive bandage around Jack's body, he said, "If that's what he be needin', suh, he'll make it. He gots plenty-a both."

"I hope so, son." Jed was surprised to detect a trace of compassion and concern sweep over the man's face. "Now you'd better hand the dog over to your friend and let us clean that bullet out of your own leg."

Jed glanced at Matt and saw that beads of sweat stood out on his forehead. "Think he's needin' yo' help first, suh," he told the officer. "I'll jes' sit here an' hold Jack."

He expected Matt to protest, but he did not. Since Matt was neither talking or complaining, Jed knew he was in bad shape. It pleased him to see Matt accept the man's hand held out in an offer of assistance. With one powerful tug, the surgeon's assistant helped Jed's friend stand up.

Since Jed had to withstand another period of waiting, he was glad to have Jack there. As always, just having the dog close to him was a comfort. Talking in a low voice near Jack's ear, he declared, "Ya's gonna be all right, boy. Gonna be fine. We's both gonna git better an' be tagethah forever." The dog never stirred. Even Matt's painful cries and moans during his surgery did not cause Dog Jack to perk up his ears.

When Matt was finally helped out of the surgical area, he was propped between the medical corpsman and an aide. Noting the look on his friend's drawn and gray face Jed was convinced that Matt must be miserable. Still silent, Matt willingly leaned against the corpsman while the aide spread out a blanket on the dirt floor. He lowered his large body onto it and heaved a great sigh. The surgeon's assistant tenderly lifted up Dog Jack and with great care placed him beside Matt on the blanket, then extended a hand to Jed and helped him to his feet — the first time Jed had tried to stand since he had plunked himself down on the ground to wait.

The pain was excruciating. Jed grimaced, but the medical man lifted Jed's arm up and around his own neck. He put his other arm around Jed's waist to give him support. Jed groaned.

"Here, boy, you can do it," the man encouraged. "Use me for a crutch and hop on your other foot."

"Yessuh," Jed replied, grateful for the physical and moral support.

He was helped into the curtained-off area and lifted onto a makeshift table. The aide cut his trouser leg completely off and began dabbing around his wound with a piece of cotton. It smarted so much that Jed's body automatically jolted and a fresh wave of apprehension surged through him. For the first time he considered what was about to happen to himself.

"Easy, son, easy," the corpsman said to Jed after his involuntary jerk. "I'm going to clean up the wound first."

Reaching into a bag he brought out a clean white cloth

and offered it to Jed. "Here, put this between your teeth and bite down hard when you think you can't stand the pain. We have to save the chloroform for amputations and we're almost out of morphine and paregoric. You can consider yourself most fortunate. The bullet is in such a place that we can most likely remove it without amputation."

Amputation! The thought sickened him. Jed closed his eyes and did as he was told, trying not to think about what the men were doing to him, but the knowledge that the surgeon would be cutting into his leg also made him squeamish. As the blade of the knife sunk deep into his flesh, he bit down on the cloth with all his might and clenched his fists until he thought his own finger nails must be slicing the palms of his hands.

Suddenly a hand closed around his left fist and Jed looked up into the kind gray-green eyes of Chaplain Stewart. The chaplain used his free hand to stroke Jed's forehead.

"Hang on to me, Jed," the chaplain coaxed. "I was so afraid I wouldn't be able to get back here in time to help you through this."

Jed's fingers grasped those of the chaplain's. As the medical men poured more alcohol on his leg, pain shot throughout his whole body. He clasped his hand tighter and tighter around Chaplain Stewart's.

"Thank God you'se heah, suh," Jed whispered through clenched teeth. Even though his words were muffled through the cloth in his mouth, Jed knew the chaplain understood, for he whispered back, "I did thank Him, Jed. Hang on a minute longer and they'll be through."

When the leg was bandaged, an aide reached down to help Jed sit up. The room whirled around him and he heard the chaplain's voice as off in a distance saying, "You go on to the next patient, I'll take care of him."

The chaplain half-carried Jed outside the surgical area to a blanket spread out on the floor beside Matt who was dozing restlessly. He put his burden down with care, then moved Dog Jack from Matt's blanket over to Jed's.

"Here, Jed, here's your friend," the chaplain said. Jed stared at the still dog lying beside him.

"Has he been movin' at all, Mistah Matt?" Jed asked.

"Not yet, Jed, but he will," Chaplain Stewart assured him in a voice filled with compassion and tenderness.

Jed looked up at his gentle friend. "Ya know, Chaplain, I don't knows how I'd ha' made it through that in there without ya. I kin never thank ya 'nough."

By that time Tom Drysdale and Bill O'Meally had made their way over to the two blankets and were standing beside Reverend Stewart.

"You don't ever need to thank me, son. All you need to do is get better so you can take care of your friend here," Chaplain Stewart said as he gestured toward Dog Jack, leaned down and lightly stroked the dog's head.

"What's the matter, boy?" he asked kindly. Dog Jack's tail seemed to move ever-so-slightly.

As Jed watched in earnest, to his great relief the tail twitched again. There was no doubt in Jed's mind!

"He's a-movin'!" Jed cried. "His tail done moved!"

With a moan Matt leaned against one elbow and tried to lift himself up high enough to see Jack. "You sure?" he asked excitedly.

The dog's tail made a complete flip from one side to the other. Both his brown canine eyes opened wide. Other men from Company F cheered with delight.

"He wagged his tail when he heard your voice, Matt!" Bill exclaimed and Matt began to both laugh and cry at the same time.

"What's the matter with him?" Bill asked.

"He's happy," Reverend Stewart answered, "because it looks like our mascot will make it after all!"

Tom Drysdale shook his head and grinned. "Can't blame you, Matt. There isn't a better mascot in the whole Union army."

The next day emergency supplies were rushed in and Matt, Jed and Dog Jack were moved to another tent with all the other ambulatory cases. Each was assigned a cot. After having to sleep on the bare ground it was a pleasure to have something a little softer on which to sleep. Jed bunked down, then lifted Dog Jack up on the cot beside him.

Matt laughed at the two resting together. "You two don't really think you're going to be bunk mates, do you?" he asked. "I'll just bet the orderly's gonna let you have a dog in bed with you! Ha!"

Jed understood Matt's point, expecting to have someone come along momentarily to order Jack down on the floor, but no one did. Jed tried to nurse his dog back to health, enticing Jack with bites from his own meals, but Jack was too weak to eat. On the second day following surgery Jed was jubilant when he successfully coaxed Dog Jack into licking some broth from a spoon.

On the third day Jed tried to get Dog Jack to stand up on his feet so he could take him outside, but Jack moaned in protest each time Jed touched him.

"All right, boy, stay here an' I'll be right beside ya till you gits better," Jed told the dog. "If ya don' feel like movin' we's not gonna leave here 'til ya do! Then..."

Before he could complete his words Chaplain Stewart rushed into the tent. The chaplain seldom showed his excitement, but from his flushed cheeks, Jed knew he was keyed up about something.

"We just received word that President Lincoln himself is coming through here!" the chaplain announced. Jed gasped along with all the other men.

"How soon, Chaplain?" George asked.

"This afternoon. He's on a tour of the battlefields and hospitals. He'll only be here a short while, so everyone who is able is supposed to gather in front of the colonel's tent in an hour."

"Hear that, boy?" Jed asked Dog Jack. "Mistah Lincoln hisself is comin' ta see us! We's gotta git ourselves over to that tent an' we'll git ta see our Pres'dent!"

Reverend Stewart was standing by Jed's cot. "I don't want to dampen your enthusiasm, son, but did it ever occur to you that Jack shouldn't be moved? Why don't you go see the President without him?"

Jed looked at the chaplain, then at the dog. "No, suh, I cain't. I promised 'im I'd stay with 'im. If he cain't go, I cain't."

"Now, Jed, you know how much you think of Mister Lincoln," the chaplain protested. "Jack won't mind you leaving him long enough to see the President of the United States of America!"

Jed refused to change his mind. No matter how the men tried to reason with him, he would not leave Jack's side. Matt kept pleading, "You're missing something you'll probably never get a chance to do again! Jed, you sure you won't give up that fool idea and come along? Jack'll probably sleep the whole time anyway."

Jed stared at the slumbering dog. For a second he felt he should, but then he declared, "I cain't, Mistah Matt. I done promised 'im."

As Matt and the others went out the door, Jed sat on his cot stroking the fur on Jack's head. "Jes' keep sleepin', boy, an' git better. That's all I really cares 'bout," he whispered to the slumbering dog, but he knew he wasn't being honest. The thought of missing out on seeing Abraham Lincoln in the flesh made him heartsick. It might be the greatest thing that ever happened to him. Everyone who could drag himself out of bed had gone off to see the President. Since he had been moved to the tent with others no longer needing constant care, they had gone to see the President and he was alone with his dog.

Jed consoled himself by continuing to pat the dog. The sound of drums and bugles outside made him aware that the men must be playing a fanfare for Mister Lincoln. The sound of men approaching aroused Jack, too, for he raised his head to look around, the most activity he'd had since the operation.

Hearing footsteps, Jed glanced toward the entrance of the tent, expecting some of the men to enter, but was astounded. A man with a black beard stooped to get through the low entrance. Once inside he stood straight and tall. Jed's eyes examined the man from his cumbersome-looking feet to his thinning black hair. Speechless for a moment, he was finally able to find enough courage to speak. "Mistah Lincoln, suh!" he gasped.

A grin began in one corner of the President's mouth and slowly filled every part of his face, especially his eyes. Then he spoke. "Chaplain Stewart said there was a soldier in here with a dog and he couldn't come to see me – so I decided to come to see them." He drawled on in his matter-of-fact way, "You must be Jed, and your friend here is Dog Jack. I hear he's quite a hero."

Jed regained enough composure to stand as best he could and salute. "Yessuh, Mistah President! Yessuh!"

Suddenly cheers rose from the men who had followed the President back to the tent. "Look at Jack!" Matt cried. Jed turned to see Dog Jack struggling to his feet – bandages and all! He stood on Jed's cot, his legs wobbling and swaying – but he STOOD! Then with an unexpected burst of energy he got down from the cot and walked outside.

Cheers for Mr. Lincoln and Jack filled the area. Jed stared at the miracle. "Mistah Lincoln," he managed to stammer, filled with emotion, "I was beginnin' ta think he'd never stand agin, but there he is. He saw you and must have known ya'd want 'im ta try. Even that dog knows you'se somebody great!" Jack had returned to Jed's side and looked up at him with an air of anticipation.

With his long thin hand, the President reached down and patted Jack's head, then faced Jed. "I thank you for your feelings, son, but no man can feel great when he sees his country broken, his men broken – or even a broken dog." Tears amassed in the President's eyes as he continued. "But I am grateful that your dog is getting better, and that you are, too."

He excused himself and turned away. Jed felt a terrible sadness as he watched him leave. "I don' knows how ya knew it, too," he told Jack, "but I thinks both of us knows we jes' met one o' the greatest men on earth."

Chapter 15
Battle at Salem Heights

The visit from President Lincoln and Dog Jack's recovery must have inspired the men of the Hundred and Second Regiment to rally to the Union cause with new enthusiasm, for as soon as they were sent back into action they fought and won numerous skirmishes and battles.

Jed overheard the men talking about the greatest stab Lee had managed to thrust into the Union's side – Robert E. Lee's forces had defeated Hooker's Union men at Chancellorsville and Lee had continued as the reinforcing source for the Southern army. From Chancellorsville Lee had strategically moved his men back to Salem Heights, Virginia, where a low range of hills covered by a forest of pine and dense undergrowth helped shelter the Rebels from the long plank road leading up to the hills.

On May 3rd, 1863, Jed and Dog Jack found themselves among the Union soldiers ordered to "Take the hill at all costs." The memory of a previous hillside battle was still too fresh in Jed's mind. As they crossed the open farm fields leading up toward the enemy stronghold, Dog Jack marched beside Jed who wondered if Jack, too, might be thinking about Malvern Hill and its consequences, or if his animal mind had been able to put such a horrible memory aside. Jed understood he would never know.

The inside of his mouth felt as dry as toast, for he realized the Rebs were lurking in the bushes on both sides.

He wished they would make a sound or give some indication of their presence. Only one thing gave Jed more chills than a stealthy, hiding, silent enemy and that was the anticipated Rebs' charge with their soul-shattering war cry, "KI-YI-KI-YI!"

The order, "SCATTER AND FLUSH THEM OUT!" came through the line and the men of the Hundred and Second entered the woods like a pack of vengeful hounds after their prey. Seconds later the same woods rolled with dense clouds of sulfurous smoke and echoed with the crack, crash and rattle of small arms. It seemed to Jed every tree, every stump had been suddenly transformed into an enemy soldier. There was no way to escape, for bayonets clashed, bullets whirred all around them. As they found their marks, men – foe and friend alike – fell to the ground. Repeatedly Jed lifted his rifle to fire. After an hour of steady volleys of gunfire back and forth, Jed reached down to reload and found, to his horror, his ammunition was nearly gone! His leg was still too weak and tender to carry him too far.

Hearing the sound of men crashing through the trees behind them he spun around, fearful that the enemy was closing in from the rear, too. He heaved a great sigh of gratitude as he saw bits of blue uniforms between the trees and knew the troops coming toward them were their own reinforcements.

Gratefully he joined the remainder of his Company F as they retraced their path back to the open field. Jed limped along, sometimes hopping to keep up with the others as they hurried past the bodies of their dead friends, leaving them unburied for fear of losing their own lives if they stopped.

"Get ready to go back in and flush them out!" the sergeant ordered and Jed sprawled on the ground with Dog Jack, waiting for the order "Follow through!" But that order never came.

Darkness closed in. Silence fell. Jed believed both sides had been forced to stop the slaughter because of sheer exhaustion. Matt searched out Jed and his dog from the others. Just as he lowered himself to the ground beside them, Jed glanced up and saw a gray uniform within a stone's throw.

"Mistah Matt!" he whispered in alarm, "a Reb!"

Matt tilted his head toward the soldier then muttered, "So what. That's his problem. If he's as tired as we are, he's too tired to shoot too. Go to sleep, Jed. My shoulder's killing me."

Matt had scarcely uttered those words when Jed glanced over to see that Matt had already followed his own suggestion. Eyes closed tightly, he'd fallen asleep.

" Sho don' know, boy," Jed whispered as he stroked the dog's head. "Don' know if I likes Rebel soldiers sleepin' near on top o' me. Gimme the spooks!"

The next morning, Monday, Jed awoke expecting a new battle to begin, but throughout the day none materialized. No action came from either side – only an ominous feeling of wondering what was about to happen. Even Dog Jack paced the ground with an air of expectancy.

Near evening Jed noticed Reverend Stewart riding toward them. One look at his unhappy countenance and Jed knew the chaplain was the bearer of bad tidings. Matt must have shared Jed's thought, for he asked, "What's the matter, sir? What is it?"

Reverend Stewart looked defeated. "I hope and pray we make it through this one, Matt. Our men captured a man carrying a dispatch from Lee. It said that half of the Southern army is closing in to capture or destroy us!"

Jed had little time to consider that statement, for their sergeant came racing through the area crying out, "Prepare! Prepare! The enemy is coming!"

Like a bolt out of the blue, the Rebs were there. Jed had never experienced more spirited fighting from the enemy. The South poured everything they had down on them. About nine in the evening the other Union corps began to retreat back through the woods, leaving Company F's men all alone, much to Jed's dismay. A break in the fighting came and the few remaining men of their company slipped over to congregate with Matt and Jed. Perched on logs and stumps, they held a council meeting, talking earnestly about what they should do.

"I don't understand," Chaplain Stewart admitted. "Obviously we were the only unit not ordered to retreat. Why would they leave us out here, cut off from the rest of the regiment?"

"Perhaps our orders never came through," the sergeant answered. "If our courier was captured or shot, we now have no choice but to attempt to make a stand here or try to get to the pontoon bridge above Fredricksburg before they do."

His words hung in mid air, for the council suddenly was brought to an abrupt halt by the familiar, yet still spine-chilling screech from out of the night, "KI-YI-KI-YI!"

Jed leaped to his feet in terror with Dog Jack following at his heels. Volley after volley of musketry barreled after them, illuminating the night as they rushed through the woods.

"Retreat! Retreat!" a voice frantically called, but there was no need for such an order. All the men were on their way.

Matt caught up with Jack and Jed. "They must have us thirty to one!" he puffed as they plummeted onward, shoving bushes and tree limbs out of their way. By then the Rebs were coming at them from the front, the rear and the left. The only remaining means of escape was through the cedar swamp off to the right.

They pushed on – sweat saturating their bodies and clothing as they crawled under bushes, jumped over tree stumps, crossed fields and waded through swampland. To save his horse from exhaustion, Reverend Stewart finally dismounted, but obviously she didn't like the move, for she lifted her hind legs, then sailed over a fence, a group of logs and finally a wide ditch. Dog Jack ran in pursuit of her, but eventually returned, panting, to the men.

"Well, I'll be," Matt declared to the chaplain, "that dumb filly of yours must think she's a fox chaser. Guess she doesn't think she's cut out for common duties such as fighting a war!"

Throughout the night the men trudged on. In the moonlight Dog Jack's eyes glistened like small yellow marbles. He whined and whimpered, limping right and left, back and forth as they pressed forward.

"I don't know, Jack, what you think we ought to do," Chaplain Stewart asked, "but you certainly don't believe in retreating, do you?"

Jed wondered if Dog Jack understood what the chaplain said, for suddenly he took off through dense undergrowth. Jed followed after him as fast as his bum leg would permit, calling, "Jack, Jack, git back heah!"

When Jed finally caught up with him he scolded, "What's ya tryin' ta do? We'll never git outa heah if we don' stay wiff the others!"

He picked Jack up and started to backtrack, in hopes of finding his fellow soldiers.

"Mistah Matt? Chaplain Stewart?" he called over and over again, but received no reply.

Momentarily he stopped to still the panic which gripped him. Petting Jack he said, "Don' worry, boy, we'll find 'em." But he wasn't sure if he was trying to console Jack or himself.

Off to the right he heard muted voices and started to carry Jack in that direction. "Matt? Chaplain?" he called again. Still he heard no answer.

"Well, Jack, we's done it. We los' Matt and the chaplain back there. We'll keep movin' 'til we finds 'em."

Placing Dog Jack on the ground he spoke with reassurance. "Don' worry, frien'. With the sun comin' up, we shouldn't has trouble findin' em." Because of his trembling knees, again he wasn't sure if he was encouraging Jack or himself.

Lifting his head, he stared into the end of a rifle barrel. "You're not going anywhere but to prison, black boy," a stern-faced Confederate soldier growled. Jed felt he was aboard a sinking ship.

Other gray-uniformed men approached, shoving and pushing Union captives in front of them, but there wasn't a man Jed knew by name among the captives.

One cocky Southern soldier who appeared to be the same age as Jed stared at Dog Jack. "That thing yours?" he drawled.

"Yessuh," Jed answered, wide-eyed with the fear of what might happen to Jack. "He be our mascot."

The fair-complexioned man, dressed in a torn Rebel uniform, lifted his rifle and pointed it down at the dog. Panic stricken, Jed quickly scooped Jack up in his arms in defiance of anyone who would harm his friend.

The soldier snickered. "I'm not proud," he sneered. "I'd just as soon shoot you both. We can't even feed ourselves, let alone two dogs!"

Although the day was warm, cold chills raced through Jed's body. He could not believe the hatred this young Southerner was showing toward him. Motionless he waited, expecting anything.

"Sergeant, drop your arms," a man in a Confederate captain's uniform ordered.

Momentarily the soldier kept his rifle pointed at the young man and his dog, then slowly dropped it to his side. "Yes, sir," he complied with reluctance. Jed knew from the sergeant's glaring eyes that only the captain's order had saved their lives. Slowly the tense muscles in Jed's face began to relax.

"We might as well take the dog along," the captain said with a grin. "Imagine how the Colonel will howl when we bring him a real dog as a prisoner!"

Minutes later the captain issued an order to march. Jed clasped Dog Jack tightly to his body in case the captain decided to change his mind. Although the extra weight caused his leg to ache, the closeness of his dog's body was a comfort.

"Don' know, boy, what we's in for," he confided to Jack. "We's done los' the chaplain an' Mistah Matt, but we still has each other."

Chapter 16
The Walls of Jericho

Jed couldn't help but think of a flock of sheep as he and the other captured soldiers were herded for several hours through the woods, then into an open field. In the clearing he was thrilled to see another band of blue-coated soldiers marching toward them.

Their attitude puzzled him, though – they were walking right up to Jed's Southern captors as though they were out on a Sunday stroll. As they neared Jed learned the reason for their seeming indifference – they were captives too!

Scanning the men's faces as they came within eyesight, he hoped he would spy one of his friends among the group. One tall, cumbersome-looking soldier towered above the others. Jed had never seen a more welcome sight.

"Mistah Matt!" he squealed. Dog Jack's ears perked up in anticipation.

A distinguished looking man with a bushy black beard was the next man in blue that Jed recognized.

"Chaplain Stewart!" he exclaimed with delight.

Then Jed recognized Jimmy Malloy. Even the sight of his old rival was a delight to him. He declared jubilantly to Dog Jack, "Now we's all tagetha agin!"

Matt and the other new captives were shoved into the group Jed was in, so Jed maneuvered his way over toward them.

"Mistah Matt!" he exclaimed, wishing he could say

more. But a rifle butt was pushed into his back and a gruff voice growled, "Keep moving, nigger!"

Dog Jack bared his teeth and snarled at the man. Jed's heart quickened. "Shush, boy," he pleaded, recognizing the voice as that of the sergeant who had wanted to shoot the "two dogs" earlier in the day.

Their band continued to march until they finally arrived at what appeared to be their destination – a long train of cattle cars.

"Get on!" the sergeant ordered while shoving aside the huge door, showing the vacant interior of a railroad car.

Jed tried to hide Dog Jack while he tugged to lift both the animal and himself into the car. When Reverend Stewart, Matt and Jimmy Malloy were aboard, he breathed more easily.

Chaplain Stewart clasped Jed's hand warmly. "Glad to see you and Jack!" the preacher declared. "When we couldn't find you, we were really concerned."

Although the walls of the cattle car were very confining for such a large group, the men sang and talked until they drifted off to sleep.

Hours later the train came to a halt and a tanned middle-aged Southern guard pulled open the door. "All right, men, we're in Annapolis. We're to make a roster of all your names and ranks, then you're being shipped to the prison at Belle Isle."

A deep penetrating silence followed that announcement. Jed knew everyone was having similar thoughts. Belle Isle was for enlisted men and noted as a most poorly kept Confederate prisoner-of-war camp. Libby, on the other hand, had been set aside for captured officers and had an even sadder reputation. Rumors had often reached Company F about the miserable way men had met their death there.

As the prisoners disembarked from the train, a sergeant barked the order, "Line up to be placed on the prisoner-of-war list." Apprehensively Jed held Dog Jack. *What were they going to do with him?* he wondered just as a stately Southern officer sauntered over. Jed recognized him as the one who had prevented the sergeant from shooting them.

"Let me hold the dog while they sign you up," he said softly. "Maybe they won't notice him then."

Jed searched the man's eyes. "Sure don' unnerstand, suh. What do ya care 'bout me an' this dog?"

The soldier stroked the top of Dog Jack's head and explained, "Y'all see, I had a dog I loved when I was a boy."

Jed shook his head in acknowledgment, waited his turn to tell his name and rank, then went over in the shadow of the railroad car to retrieve Dog Jack from the officer.

He offered his gratitude: "Thank ya, suh."

The man replied, "I think you can keep him now. Try to keep him quiet, though." With that, he strode away.

Reverend Stewart approached Jed. "See you found a friend in the enemy camp," he whispered.

"Yessuh," Jed replied. Before he could say more, Matt was beside them, waving his arms and talking excitedly to the chaplain. "You're crazy, Reverend! I heard them offer you your freedom and you wouldn't take it!"

Jed stared open-mouthed at the preacher. "Reveren' Stewart, why din't ya take it?"

Looking straight into Jed's eye the chaplain answered, "I couldn't. My job is to stay with my men." Then turning to Matt he smiled and added, "And you, you're one of them."

"I still think you're loco," Matt grumbled. There was no time for further discussion, for they were herded back into the cattle cars and were on their way once more, this time with no doubt in their minds as to where they were going and what to expect.

Toward morning the train doors were pulled open and the captives were aroused from their sleep by a Southern officer's announcement, "This is Belle Isle. Your quarters are in that building to the right. Step to it. This train is needed immediately for transporting our own troops."

Even though the sun was rising, Jed had never seen a more dismal looking compound. Something about the gray-looking buildings with their streaks of ancient whitewash and penetrating odors made him feel squeamish inside.

Jed clasped Dog Jack even more tightly as they were led through the compound and over to the gray shed which had been assigned to them. The sights were soul shattering as they passed by barred rooms – thin, fragile faces stared up at them through hollow eyes.

"Good Lord!" Chaplain Stewart declared, "You are needed here!" Jed had to agree. Something or someone certainly was needed. He decided that surely that hole must be the end of the world.

Even Matt's face grew more drawn and peaked. His eyes darted about as they entered the small wooden building with only one tiny barred window. Never in the heat of any battle had Jed ever seen Matt's eyes so fearful as now, when eight men were squeezed into such small quarters.

"We haven't enough food to keep body and soul together," the short, pudgy guard announced, "so you'll get meager rations twice a day. You will be closely guarded. Don't try to escape, because we enjoy having one less mouth to feed."

Turning to leave, the guard's squinting eyes came to rest on Dog Jack. "What's that?" he demanded, trying his best to stand tall.

"Company mascot, suh!" Jed answered, his heart weighing heavily inside his chest.

"We can't feed him!" the guard snorted and added curtly, "If you want him to live, you'll have to share your rations – and I doubt if either of you can survive."

In the days that followed Jed found out what the term "meager rations" meant – a spoonful of rice broth twice a day in a filthy battered tin cup. Occasionally they were served crackers. The first time the guards gave them these new rations, Jed was pleased until he realized what the black spots in the little squares really were. "Worms!" he cried as his stomach convulsed. But soon he learned to ignore the moving creatures. He was too starved to dare to take notice.

Matt and the Malloy boy became the chaplain's and Jed's prime concerns. Jed had never thought about what Matt might do in captivity, but he soon found out. As days, weeks and months passed, Matt paced the floor like a caged tiger.

Having too little to do, too much to think about, and being penned in too confining a space was hard on Matt. He began having nightmares, crying aloud as he slept. When Chaplain Stewart comforted him as he would a small child, Matt would drift back into a restless sleep.

Jimmy Malloy became more pale and thin by the day. With alarm the chaplain confided in Jed, "Young Jimmy's really ill. If he doesn't get out of here soon, I don't think he'll make it."

Dog Jack had been their sole stabilizer up to that point. At first he had amused the men with his tricks. He seemed to sense whenever one of them became excessively discouraged and would go overboard showing off for them – walking on his hind legs and pretending to beg. But after months in captivity the men completely lost their sense of humor and Dog Jack became too weak to perform. Malnutrition, hunger and frustration had taken away all enthusiasm and zeal.

One morning Matt rose early and started his usual pacing back and forth, back and forth. Suddenly he started to pound the wall frantically and scream, "I'd rather die! I'd rather die!"

Jed and Dog Jack stared at their friend, but Chaplain Stewart moved to Matt's side, saying in a soothing voice, "Matt, Matt, you don't mean it."

Jed watched with anguish as his big friend crumbled. His once mighty form looked diminished and pitiful as he sobbed uncontrollably in the chaplain's arms. "We'll never get out! We'll never get out!" he wailed over and over. Matt buried his head down in the chaplain's lap.

"Yes, we will, Matt" Chaplain Stewart promised. "Nothing's impossible. Even the great walls of Jericho finally tumbled and we have nothing so great surrounding us. We must pray and have patience."

Matt lifted his head. Tears streamed down his face as he cried, "My baby's almost a year old and I've never seen my own child. I'll never see her!"

"Yes, you will, Matt," the chaplain assured him. "Just pray. Pray for patience."

After his outburst, Matt appeared to be in a better frame of mind, but Jed could see Jimmy Malloy was becoming physically weaker and weaker. Obviously their chaplain was growing more concerned, and Jed found another problem to worry about. Fear had gnawed at his heart when he heard Tom Drysdale whispering to George Brown, "Without that dog we'd have more food!"

For a few moments, his fellow prisoner's statement made no impact, but then terror gripped him. "Reverend Stewart," he whispered, "they's talkin' 'bout Jack!"

The chaplain shook his head. "I heard, Jed. I think it's time I took Jimmy and Dog Jack out of here. I hate to leave you and Matt, but young Jimmy's not going to live unless he gets proper care soon."

Jed was aghast at the preacher's idea. "How's ya gonna do it, suh?" he asked.

"The North has sick and wounded prisoners that the South wants returned, too. They'll move us out of here for exchange."

"And Matt?" Jed asked. "How kin ah reckon with Mistah Matt? You knows best how to handle 'im!" Jed insisted.

The chaplain pushed Jed's curly hair back on his head. Jed recognized this gesture as one of affection. "Don't worry, son. Matt'll be all right now. He's got more stamina than he thinks, and I'm sure his outburst the other morning helped him work some of his frustrations out of his system."

The next day Jed observed anxiously as Chaplain Stewart talked to one of the guards, then followed him out of their cell. Jed knew his beloved friend the chaplain, a most convincing talker, was probably speaking to the authorities. He was not surprised to see the chaplain, when he returned, immediately begin to pack Jimmy Malloy's belongings.

"Ya really gonna go?" Jed inquired of him, startled to find the words sticking in his throat.

"They said we can leave tonight. I tried to impress them with the gravity of Jimmy's condition. It's almost six months to the day since we arrived here."

"Ya takin' Jack, too?" Jed asked, trying not to sound anxious.

"Yes, Jed. They're exchanging Jack for a Confederate prisoner. Guess the Union knows a good soldier after all!"

"Chaplain Stewart, take good care of 'im, please," Jed pleaded. The thought of having Jack taken away sickened him.

The chaplain placed a consoling arm around Jed's shoulders. "Don't worry, boy. Jack'll be fine in Pittsburgh. I'll take him to Molly to keep her company. You take care of Matt and yourself."

That night Jed stood with Matt in the doorway as the Confederate guards carried Jimmy Malloy out on a stretcher. Reverend Stewart turned and grasped Jed's hand, then Matt's.

"God bless you and keep you both," the chaplain said, his voice filled with emotion. Neither could find words to respond.

"Come on, Jack," Reverend Stewart called. Jack looked inquiringly at Jed and Matt as if trying to figure out what to do.

"Go — go, boy," Jed managed to say, remembering his mother's urgent plea the day he escaped from a life of slavery. With his heart aching, he watched as Dog Jack followed the chaplain from the dingy room.

Jed felt that life itself had been drained from him. He stared at the door, fighting the panic and desperation which was waging war within his whole being. For six months he'd had his canine companion right by his side. In an instant he was gone. Jed wondered how he'd handle confinement without him.

The expression on his friend Matt's face convinced Jed that the chaplain was right. Matt obviously was over the hump, although Jed couldn't say the same for himself.

"The chaplain says even the great walls of Jericho tumbled down, Jed boy. Maybe if we believe strongly enough we'll get out of this stinking hole too." Matt's consoling tone surprised Jed.

Days passed by and time dragged its hands across the face of Matt's small pocket watch. One morning the pudgy guard they had come to detest announced, "Get your gear packed. Today's exchange day. We're shipping you North this afternoon."

For a brief moment the men stared at each other in disbelief. Then a wild cheer of jubilation filled the room. Even Tom Drysdale rose to his feet and wept with sheer joy.

A Union officer in his welcome blue uniform came for them. They boarded a train and — suddenly they were free! Even the air smelled different to Jed. He breathed deeply as he stared out the window of the passenger coach. The ties which had bound him had been cut loose and he wished that Dog Jack and Reverend Stewart could have shared that precious and joyous time with him.

When the train pulled into Pittsburgh, Jed glanced all around. Other men of Company F and their families were there waiting. Jed drank in the sight, overjoyed to see his friends once more. A band played "The Battle Hymn of the Republic" to welcome them home.

Matt and Jed were still standing on the station platform when Jed looked up and could not believe his eyes.

Reverend Stewart stood beside his mare. He was holding Dog Jack.

"Dog Jack!" Jed shouted. His dog yelped in delight, jumped from the chaplain's arms and raced to Jed.

Dog Jack lapped at Jed's face, whining with enthusiasm. He jumped down, raced around and around in a circle, then leaped back up into Jed's arms. Jed laughed uncontrollably as he watched the antics of the dog unable to contain its joy.

"Molly!" he heard Matt cry out above the noise and excitement. Glancing up, he saw Molly clutching a squirming blond-headed little girl while running toward Matt. Matt wasted no time in reaching them, then swooped both of them up into his arms.

Molly and Matt stood entwined together, swaying with laughter and tears, their small daughter caught in the middle of their embrace.

After all the horrible sights and sounds he had witnessed, Jed's heart warmed as he watched that joyous reunion. He relished the comfort of his beloved dog in his arms once again. Even though he knew they soon would have to leave Pittsburgh because there was still a war to fight, fleeting moments such as this still made life worth living.

Men look to the clergy.

Chapter 17
Gratitude for a Hero

On the train ride to Pittsburgh Matt had surprised Jed with a suggestion. "You know, no one ever had a mascot as great as our Dog Jack! We ought to do something special to let the world see how we feel about him – maybe get him a real silver collar."

"A silver collar?" Jed echoed. "Do ya knows how much one costs?" He rolled his eyes. "Mistah Matt, we nevah, evah could afford one!"

Matt's head shook in disagreement. "You're wrong, son. We could have ourselves a ball and raise the money."

Jed studied Matt's words before he asked his next question; he didn't want to look foolish, but wasn't sure what Matt meant by "having a ball." Cautiously he inquired, "Ya meanin' a real live dance where folks dress up in them fancy clothes?"

A smug smile of satisfaction crossed Matt's face. Jed knew the wheels of his friend's mind were already churning with plans to put this idea into action. But then the train arrived at Pittsburgh and, after all the hoopla of their arrival and the seeing of his baby for the first time, Jed assumed that Matt had probably forgotten his scheme to make Jack a celebrity. Impetuous, his big buddy often made big plans one minute and forgot them the next.

Not so that time. The next day the former fire chief wandered into the station, gently pulling Molly in tow with his right hand and baby Rebecca carefully tucked inside his left arm. Jed couldn't help but be a little amused at the contrast in size between father and daughter. After first cooing over his offspring, Matt came right to the point of his visit. "We'd better get going on the plans for the ball, or we'll have to be getting back to war without anything ever happening to honor our mascot. After all – he saved my life."

Matt's words amused Jed. Didn't he ever remember how the dog had been the butt of his temper tantrums; how he'd thought of banishing him from the fire hall the first moment he saw him? Evidently not, for at that moment his total concern was to officially proclaim Dog Jack a hero.

"Don' know nothin' 'bout dances, Mistah Matt. The only ones I ever had much ta do with, I only got ta watch the Southern ladies an' their gents show up in their spiffy clothes. What I 'member most was that my pappy had ta stay up all night long sometimes, fixin' fancy foods for them folks in their finery."

Molly, who had been listening in silence, piped up with her suggestions. "You're going to have to get a hall first, so we can make up the tickets and some posters. If you find the place, Matt, I'll do the rest."

"I want to make at least seventy-five dollars profit," Matt bragged. "That'll get our dog the finest collar there is!"

His goal overwhelmed Jed. "Seventy-five dollars!" he cried. "That's a heap o' money ta waste on a dog!"

"WASTE?" Matt bellowed, the familiar tinge of red coloring his ear lobes. Jed knew it would be wise to keep any further opinions to himself. When his big friend reacted like a burning ember, it didn't take a lot of fanning to cause him to burst into flame.

Instead of pushing his luck, Jed decided to choose another line of questioning. "Where do ya think we could have the ball?"

"Downtown – in the most elegant place we can find."

Jed agreed. "Good ideer, but we's surely gonna have ta find a big place if we's gonna raise big money."

Molly giggled. "That's no problem with him, Jed. He

always thinks big." With adoration she looked up at her husband. Jed could see Matt was the major focus in the life of his wife.

With fervor Matt started out on his search for a large hall and returned that same day claiming, "I got us Lafayette Hall right here in downtown Pittsburgh. It'll hold five hundred guests. — could hold more, but women in those silly hoop skirts take up a lot of room."

Once the place was decided upon, Matt called all the Niagara Volunteers together for a meeting at the fire hall. Cribbage tournaments had caused a flurry of excitement, but nothing had ever enthused the men as much as this project to honor their mascot. "We can do it!" their leader claimed. "We can fill the hall for twenty-five cents a person. Our wives can bake their favorite cookies. We can have tea and punch. Chaplain Stewart would never approve of serving liquor."

Jed glanced at the chaplain whose face was beaming with approval.

"Three cheers for Dog Jack!" Matt cried.

The men rose to their feet, raising their glasses and cups as if to propose a toast.

"Hurrah! Hurrah! Hurrah! Three cheers for Dog Jack!" The name of their canine war hero echoed through the fire station. The cheering was interrupted by a loud "Ha!" from Tom Drysdale, pointing to the floor area in front of Jed. All eyes followed his gesture.

Their mascot, the one they were cheering with such fervor, had fallen asleep at Jed's feet during the planning meeting where he'd been proclaimed a total hero. At the sound of his name, his ears perked up, he opened one drowsy eye, then the other.

"Hurrah for Dog Jack!" the men cheered again. Jack responded by rising to his feet. Immediately he stood tall and straight as if he were at attention. A wave of laughter crossed through the firehouse as the men watched the antics of their favorite war hero.

"Let's get to work, fellows," Matt encouraged. "We can

make this event one that Pittsburgh will never forget. Drop by tomorrow after lunch and Molly will have the tickets ready."

After the firehouse cleared, Jed found himself alone with Matt and Chaplain Stewart. Gathering courage, he finally asked, "Mistah Matt, don' I even git ta come ta the ball?"

Caught off guard, Matt stood speechless for a moment – a rarity in his life. At last he replied, "Course you can, Jed. Guess you could help the women in the kitchen."

Jed felt as though his face had been slapped. *HELPS THE WIMMIN IN THE KITCHEN!* The words raced through his mind. He'd been man enough to go to war as a soldier in the Union Army, but he wasn't considered man enough to go to a ball honoring HIS dog! "Mistah Matt," he protested, "I'd rather see the ball."

Matt looked perplexed. As if thinking aloud, he said, "But, Jed, who'd be your partner? What would you wear?"

Chaplain Stewart looked solemnly at Jed, then spoke to Matt, "I think the logic is simple. Jed's really Dog Jack's master, and we could hardly have a ball without the honoree. Jed could come in his uniform and take charge of Jack for the evening."

"That's a great idea!" Matt exclaimed with a sigh of relief.

Dog Jack barked as if he agreed with their decision.

"Matt," the chaplain added, "Jed's here all the time. Why not put him in charge of the tickets? I'll make a roster of the men and he can have them sign beside their names how many tickets they take and how many they've sold. He's really learned his numbers and how to figure money."

"Fine with me. How about you, Jed?" Matt asked.

"Ya mean I'd be in charge o' all the money?" Jed questioned.

"We don't have a more trustworthy soul," Chaplain Stewart added. "We'll just depend on you to take charge. Is that all right?"

"Yes, suh – if ya think I can do it."

"I know you can," the preacher assured him.

Later, when Jed and Dog Jack were about to bed down for the night in the stable loft, Jed told his canine companion, "Ya know, Jack, when God made folks, he had ta plan on purpose for Chaplain Stewart ta be one o' the mos' special of all."

Chapter 18
Staging the Ball

When ticket sales soared, Matt's enthusiasm soared with them. "We're going to reach our goal!" he cried.

Jed studied for a moment, then asked out of curiosity, "Mistah Matt, why seventy-five dollars?"

Sheepishly, Matt answered, "Before we even marched off to war, I spied this grand collar in Mr. Payne's store – all etched and everything. He told me because it had a seventy-five dollar price tag, he never expected to sell it. But I'm out to prove him wrong."

So that was the reason. Matt always took the impossible as a personal challenge.

By Wednesday evening, the tickets were gone, so Molly was given the added responsibility of seeing to the refreshments. Plans were progressing without a hitch. Jed busied himself on Friday by putting the stable in order and making sure his uniform was without spot or wrinkle, giving Dog Jack a bath at the last minute. "Ya might not like this, fella," Jed consoled the wriggling dog, "but I's gonna make sure ya looks like a hero!"

That clear and cool August evening Jed and Dog Jack went to Lafayette Hall early. George Brown had rounded up a fiddler, a banjo player and a pianist. Music drifted from the hall before any of the paying guests arrived. Some of the Niagara Volunteers had offered the services of their young offspring to collect tickets. Jed noticed that the youngsters were already "having a ball" as they swirled around in their fancy clothes in time to the pre-ball music.

Suddenly guests began to arrive. Their elegant apparel caused Jed to think that perhaps he was living in a fairy tale. Women swished their skirts and chatted with friends. Most of the men stood by and watched with admiration. Jed sensed they were all pleased with their women folk.

Older ladies sat on the sidelines behind their fans and whispered to one another as the musicians began to play tunes appropriate for dancing. The guests waltzed and curtsied, drank from dainty cups around the punch bowl and ate the delicacies set before them while Jed stood in the corner with the hero of the day. No one seemed to pay much attention to the mascot of the Pennsylvania 102nd Regiment who stood by watching curiously as though he'd never seen such goings on.

While convalescing in a hospital after his left leg had been amputated, one of the men in the regiment had painted a portrait of Jack. That picture had been framed and placed outside the large main door at the front of the hall along with a sign which read, "BENEFIT BALL TONIGHT. Proceeds to buy a silver collar for DOG JACK – mascot of the Pittsburgh Volunteers." Even so, the participants paid him little heed, which bothered Jed.

"Jack, jes' look at 'em. They paid good money ta come ta a ball in yo' honor – but no one seems ta care if you'se even here."

Jed's lament had barely escaped his mouth when Chaplain Stewart came by. "There you are!" he declared. "Jed, nobody's going to see our hero if you stay off in a corner with him."

"But, Chaplain Stewart – what ya want me ta do?"

"It won't be long till the gala evening runs down. Matt's asked me to present the collar to Dog Jack then and say a few appropriate words. Jed, something else's bothering you, isn't it?"

"Yessuh. I wasn't jes' thinkin' 'bout Jack. I've been watchin' all this frivolity an' wonderin' how ever'one kin be laughin' and happy when men's dyin' on the battlefield an' thousands o' others are losin' limbs or eyesight. Sure don' feel like celebratin' when I stop ta think 'bout wha's happenin' all over the country. Makes me feel guilty havin' a ball with so much misery goin' on. Look at that black man on stage singin' 'Old Black Joe' and listen ta all the music and dancin' and laughin'. I cain't unnerstand."

For a moment, Chaplain Stewart stroked his beard. "Jed, you think that all those people out there dancing are pleased about the war?"

"Oh, no, suh. Doubt if there's one who don' care, but why's they havin' such a gay time?"

"Jed, Jed! Heaven knows many men and women from this American generation have been deprived of family life and normal living – don't deprive folks of one night of gaiety. I just received a telegram saying we have to start back to the front late Sunday afternoon. Who wants to face that?"

Jed's eyes roamed the big hall. "Nobody heah – that's fo' sho'."

"Matt'll call for Jack in a few minutes so our mascot can have his moment of glory. After that I'm going to close with a song. Then I have to do what I must, even though I know it'll spoil the whole evening. I'll have to announce that we'll be moving out Sunday. The men must have time to ready themselves."

Even with lightheartedness surrounding him, Jed felt a wave of apprehension. They were going back to the front! Truly it had been easy to forget the misery of war in the short time they had been home.

Matt walked toward him, beaming with pleasure. "Jed, come on. Bring Jack out here for everyone to see!"

Jed obliged. As the mascot appeared center stage the crowd went into an uproar. "Hurrah! Hurrah! Hurrah for Dog Jack!" To Jed the noise sounded more like a thunder clap than a cheer. He would have liked to plug his ears. The men of the regiment hurried to the stage and took positions behind the honored mongrel.

As Matt unwrapped a beautiful package and pulled out the elegant silver collar, the cheering subsided and oohs and aahs filled the hall. The regiment's mascot stood like a celebrated soldier receiving a medal of honor as Matt buckled the collar around his neck.

"Three more cheers!" Matt hollered. Once more the thunderous cheer echoed through the hall. Matt's face became solemn.

Everyone grinned for an instant as Matt spoke his rehearsed speech in words so unlike him: "We give this token of esteem to you, Dog Jack, for all your valiant efforts on behalf of the 102nd Regiment. The Niagara Volunteers salute you." Hearing those words, the men who'd gone to war with the dog snapped to attention and saluted the animal with as much respect as they would have had for a visiting general.

Matt turned to the chaplain and said, "Sir, we'd like you to adjourn this gathering. Ladies and gentlemen, this is Rev. A.M. Stewart whose valor and courage and faith have made him one of the greatest chaplains in the Union Army. President Lincoln himself should send him a commendation for his integrity and worth."

Applause filled the room as the chaplain rose to speak. "Friends and neighbors, I am deeply grateful for this evening and for the reason we have come together. Even though our mascot is only an animal, he has added life to our unit. He has literally rescued men from the ravages of war by his acts of courage. And so I am pleased to honor him.

"Yet this very night there are men who are engaged in skirmishes and hand-to-hand fighting. Some are dying. Some wish they were dead. In honor of those brave soldiers and those of us who will go to rejoin the unit this Sunday night, I would like for all of you to join me in singing 'The Battle Hymn of the Republic.'"

Matt couldn't have been more shocked if he'd been hit with a lightning bolt. "Wait! Wait just a minute, sir. Do you mean that we're going back on Sunday?" The frantic pleading tone in his voice caused Jed to think HE'S SAYING DO*N'T LET IT BE SO!*

All eyes were on the chaplain. His words affected each one present – of that Jed was certain.

"Afraid so, Matt. We knew it was coming. It just came sooner than we would have liked. God brought us this far, He'll get us the rest of the way."

Sobriety replaced their gaiety. As Jed looked around the room he realized each person was thinking of the consequences of more war and separation.

The musicians began to play and the crowd joined in, "Mine eyes have seen the glory of the coming of the Lord. He has trampled out the vineyards where the grapes of wrath are stored...." By the time "His truth is marching on" was sung, only a few of those gathered were able to continue to sing. Women had turned to their husbands to embrace. Even some of the men sobbed openly. Dog Jack, at Jed's feet, whimpered as if the whole situation was too much for him. For Jed, that moment was another one of those times when he felt so alone.

He glanced down and stretched out his hands. The dog literally jumped into his open arms. Once more Jed felt as though he belonged to someone.

Silently and solemnly people streamed out of the ballroom, women clinging to their husbands, men's faces piqued and drawn. Little time was left for them to prepare. As Jed and Dog Jack walked alone to the hay loft to bed down for the night, Jed leaned down to pat his dog friend. "Well, they shuh 'nuf made ya a hero fo' a minute anyways. Too bad the evenin' had ta end this way."

Later Jed snuggled close to Dog Jack. "Hate ta think what we's in fo' next." With those words both drifted off to sleep.

On Sunday evening Jed and Dog Jack watched as men streamed in from all directions to board the six o'clock train.

As they fell into line, Jimmy Malloy stood at the front, beating his drum. Jed noticed he no longer looked like a boy, but more like a seasoned soldier. His mother turned her head, otherwise she would have been unable to let him go again.

They'd all experienced so much in the war, each was repulsed by the thought of returning. Nevertheless, each man kissed his family members hurriedly and boarded the train.

The whistle blew. Jed and Dog Jack stared out the window. Women and children waved as the train pulled out of the station. The men of the 102nd, returning to the front, rode south, regretful about leaving home and fearful of what was to come.

Chapter 19
River Bank Revival

After their all-too-brief reprieve Company F was back at the front, back eating rations of hard tack and salt pork – when they were lucky. Jed observed the other soldiers as the regiment marched along side the Rappahannock River in Virginia. Their complaints, their whines were familiar sounds. He knew all too well how tired and hungry they really were, for he, too, had lived on half-rations for so long he could hardly remember when he hadn't felt a hollow feeling in the depths of his stomach – even after he had eaten. When hunger got the best of the men, they even resorted to shooting robins and cooking them over an open fire into a stew.

Dog Jack usually fared far better than the men, even though he didn't carry a pack as the others did – he didn't have to. Jed doubted that there was a man in Company F who didn't share a part of each meal with Jack – nothing more than a morsel from each man, but all their little tidbits added up to a full meal.

Jack often contributed to their meals in return, for he was an exceptional hunter. If an unsuspecting rabbit or squirrel wandered too close to Jack's jaws, Company F had fresh meat on a spit for dinner.

One rabbit or one squirrel furnished each soldier with little more than a taste, but it always seemed to Jed that Reverend Stewart made the most of such small blessings. On occasions when there was fresh meat the chaplain gave extra thanks during grace for the Lord's abundant blessing. Jed thought it rather strange to thank Someone they couldn't see for something he felt Dog Jack had actually provided.

As they moved along, Jed began to sing the new words that a woman named Julia Ward Howe had written to the tune of "John Brown's Body". The chaplain had copied them down when he had been to a prayer meeting with the 24th New Jersey Regiment and had brought them back for the men of the Hundred and Second to learn.

Jed had taken to them easily. He enjoyed singing to the accompaniment of Tom Drysdale's harmonica as they marched along. The other men joined in as soon as Jed and the chaplain had sung the words a couple of times:

> "We'll soon light our fires on the
>   Rappahannock shore –
> We'll soon light our fires on the
>   Rappahannock shore –
> And tell Father Abraham he needn't call for more –
> While we go marching on."

They had just begun to sing the second line when a mournful wail rose up from the midst of the men. For a second, the sound startled Jed until he looked at Matt who nearly doubled over with laughter. Jack was marching alongside Matt – his head tilted way back and his mouth opened wide, pouring forth the most woeful sound Jed had ever heard – except for the times he had overheard Matt gargling with salt water to overcome a sore throat.

Tears of glee streamed down Matt's face. "I've never heard anything so funny in my life!" he managed to spit out between fits of laughter. "That crazy dog thinks he's singing!"

The other men joined in the hilarity and when their own singing stopped, Jack's wailing ceased, too. He glanced around at the men, then turned his head away from them, marching with his nose upward as if his pride had been injured.

"Ah, come on, Jack! Sing!" Matt coaxed, but Dog Jack refused.

Even Chaplain Stewart who never made fun of anybody had to laugh at Dog Jack's antics. With a pat on Jack's head, he declared, "Well, you can't say you don't participate one hundred per cent in all company functions, can you?"

Jed grinned and patted the dog, too, but Jack moved away from him. Jed chortled. "Don' pout, ya silly dog!"

Matt chuckled, "You're the world's worst singer, but you've given us the best laugh we've had in a long time!"

The Hundred and Second and their mascot continued to march, but no amount of pleading from anyone — not even from Chaplain Stewart — would entice Jack to sing again. He seemed to resent their having made fun of him.

Matt hooted with delight, "I think we've wounded his dignity. I've never seen such artistic temperament in a dog."

It was a good thing Dog Jack had provided them with some amusement, for in the months that followed they found little to laugh at. Days were growing colder, the men's sore feet were rebelling more because of their long, long march. Hunger pangs became a part of their make-up. Jed watched sadly as best friends fought over scraps of meat, as tempers flared between men who had never before exchanged harsh words.

Chaplain Stewart was the only one able to remain calm during those trying days. No matter what misery befell them, the chaplain managed to stay cheerful and offer the right words at the right times, causing Jed to often wonder how this man he admired retained his tranquillity so effectively.

For a while, even Dog Jack appeared to have let them down. He hadn't been providing much meat for their dinners because he had found a preoccupation to replace his hunting.

Ever since Dog Jack had first sighted Pollyanna, the small white terrier mascot of the 93rd Regiment, he had paid little attention to any of his soldierly duties. One morning Jed watched enviously as Jack and his lady friend romped through the big weeds. At first Jed had been amused, but his amusement turned into alarm when Jack refused to heed his call for the first time since they had been together.

Jed had stood on the hillside watching Jack and Pollyanna frolic near the river bank until he had decided it was time to move on. He called down to the dog below, "Here, Jack. Time to go, boy." But Pollyanna ran behind a thicket and Jack followed. All Jed could see was the tips of their tails wagging above the weeds.

The two disappearing dogs caused mixed emotions for Jed. At first he felt anger that Jack had ignored him, then jealousy and fear lest he might be losing the prime spot in Dog Jack's life.

"That's what I call high-tailing it," said an amused and familiar voice. Jed turned to face Chaplain Stewart and knew immediately because of the chaplain's next statement that his preacher friend was well aware of his feelings. "Don't worry, Jed, he's infatuated right now, but he'll be back and be all yours again soon. Have a little patience and he'll get over wooing Pollyanna."

Jed grinned. "Silly thing ta be worryin' 'bout, suh – how a dog feels 'bout another dog," he admitted in shame.

Reverend Stewart clasped him across the back. "Not really, son," he consoled, "not when that dog's the most important thing in your life. Jealousy, on the other hand, is something to fight off. It's something that can eat the heart right out of you if you let it stick around."

Chaplain Stewart turned to go back with the others, but Jed stood momentarily looking for Jack and Pollyanna. Seeing neither, he joined the chaplain with reluctance. Later on in the evening Jed glanced up from his supper and saw Dog Jack racing toward him.

Jed reached down and lifted the dog up in his arms. Jack greeted him by lapping at his face and Jed smiled. He felt intact once more. Glancing over at Reverend Stewart, his eyes met the chaplain's. Without even uttering a word, the chaplain winked a knowing wink to acknowledge Dog Jack's predicted return.

Mail call that day was the first in two weeks. How difficult it was for the mail to keep up with a troop on the move.

That night at the campfire many of the men were talking together about the letters the carrier had delivered to them earlier in the afternoon. The morale of those who had received letters was much higher than before, but from observing the downcast appearance of several of his colleagues, Jed decided it might have been better if no one had heard from home. No one ever wrote to him. Who of his family was left to write?

Matt was one of the men who didn't receive any mail. Despondent from not hearing from Molly or his family, he stayed in the background brooding. Tom Drysdale hit the jackpot, receiving three pieces of mail. In a gay mood, Tom blew the scale on his harmonica each time he opened a letter.

"Hey, Matt," he called over his shoulder. "Worried that old Molly girl's stepping out on you?"

The mocking tone in his voice was evident. Matt didn't answer, but tore around in front of the row of men sitting on a long log and grabbing hold of the front of Tom's shirt, lifted him off his seat. By the orange-yellow light from the fire Jed could see Matt's face. His expression frightened him. He had seen Matt's tense look and clenched jaw before and knew they spelled trouble.

"What do you KNOW?" Matt demanded. Tom crumbled in Matt's hands.

"Matt, I was just teasing! HONEST!" he protested, raising his arms in a futile attempt to protect himself from the angry man who was much larger than himself.

Prancing back and forth, barking at one and then the other, Dog Jack tried to figure out what his friends were doing.

"Whoa, Matt! Whoa!" Chaplain Stewart cried as Matt pulled his huge right arm back to deliver a wallop. "Can't you believe he was only kidding?"

When Matt lowered his arm, then slowly placed Tom back onto his seat, Jed breathed more easily. He hadn't considered before what pent-up emotions, what worries Matt must have been having about Molly, but he could see then that Tom had hit a sore spot with his jesting. Even though he had put Tom down, Matt's face still seethed with anger.

The chaplain moved between the two men. "Don't you think the two of you need to reconsider your wrath and shake hands like the friends you really are?"

Tom, much smaller than Matt, extended his hand to his upset buddy. "I'm sorry, Matt. I didn't really think how it sounded. I don't know anything about your wife."

Matt made no move to accept Tom's gesture of good will, so Chaplain Stewart prodded him, "Come on, Matt. It's not like you to refuse to forgive somebody. Shake hands with your friend."

Matt's reluctance was evident as he slowly forced his hand toward Tom, but Tom reached out and grasped it eagerly. "I really am sorry, Matt. It was a stupid thing to say." Matt's sullen mood did not fade quickly.

Chaplain Stewart tactfully initiated the singing of some hymns, but Matt refused to join in. The absence of his lusty bass voice was noticed by his companions. On most occasions he loved to open his mouth wide and let the notes roll out, filling the air with song; but not that night. Often Chaplain Stewart asked Matt to lead the songs, but on this occasion he decided it would be wise to allow Matt to sit and sulk and watch the campfire undisturbed. Dog Jack lay at Matt's feet, looking up at him curiously as if he were wondering what ailed him.

Harry Svetland reached down, gave Dog Jack a gentle pat on the head and declared, "You're the best doggone mascot in the whole Union army!"

Harry's compliment brought a thought to Matt's mind which broke his sullen mood. He chuckled. "Doggone you anyway, Jack! Speaking of mascots, there's some strange ones around! Heard tell the other day about an eagle that a Wisconsin regiment hauls around with them. They call it, 'Old Abe' – I reckon after President Lincoln. A soldier from their regiment claimed it gets all excited when the shooting gets wild and it flutters its wings and tries to be as noisy as the artillery." Matt's chuckle turned into a howl. "It gave its owners the surprise of their life one day. That eagle got so blamed excited that it showed its true colors and laid an egg. 'Old Abe' wasn't so fitting for a name after all!"

Tom Drysdale piped up, "Didn't you fellows ever hear about the Saint Bernard – you know, one of those giant dogs – that was wailing over a fallen soldier? The men of the regiment that found him took him along and adopted him for a mascot of their own."

George added, "But the wildest tale I ever heard about a mascot was one about the Southern officer who rode into Gettysburg with a fox on his shoulder and a coonskin cap on his head. Had his band playing 'Dixie', but, realizing their blunder, they changed to 'Yankee Doodle.'" The men all laughed.

As Jed observed their short-lived merriment, he decided laughter was like a merry medicine just as Chaplain Stewart had once said.

Tom raised his harmonica to his lips and started playing "Dixie." Seconds later Matt was up and chasing him around the campfire, Dog Jack barking wildly at his heels.

"Just jesting, Matt!" Tom cried and settled down to playing more serious tunes – songs Jed had heard the men sing around the old upright piano in the fire hall.

Back in Pittsburgh they'd sung the tunes with real gusto, but as they sat staring into the campfire, he noticed a touch of melancholy in the voices as they sang, "Weeping, Sad and Lonely"..."Mother Kissed Me in My Dreams" and "The Girl I Left Behind Me." Jed felt no nostalgia, for he had no living mother, no girl friend. Yet he could understand their feelings and wished he still had someone – somewhere – longing to see him again.

While the men were singing "Tenting Tonight" a courier rode in, dismounted from his horse, then strode over to the chaplain. "Chaplain, sir," he reported, "here's five pieces of mail which were accidentally sent to our regiment. We know what mail means to the men, so I brought them over tonight."

Chaplain Stewart held them up to the light of the fire so he could make out the names. Smiling, he handed Matt two of the letters. "Here, Matt. It looks like these belong to you."

Matt's face was illuminated, and the whole group brightened along with him. As Matt and three others opened their letters, Jed threw some logs on the dying fire — even the fire seemed to burst forth with new enthusiasm. The men began to sing hymns of praise while Matt read his mail. Then he joined in the singing with great gusto, his tremendous voice adding impact to the words, "Mine eyes have seen the glory of the coming of the Lord."

The chaplain rose from his sitting position in the center of the group seated on logs around the campfire and announced, "I feel moved to pray to God Almighty and thank Him for His many blessings to us and ask Him for guidance in the days to come. Those who wish may add their own thanks and put their own petitions before the Lord."

Every man rose to his feet. As their chaplain progressed with his prayer, a strange hush, a feeling of awe Jed had never experienced at any other meeting fell across the group. There was no sound except the crackling of the campfire and the voice of the company chaplain. Jed glanced around. Every head was bowed. Even Dog Jack was sitting on his haunches and his head was lowered as if he, too were praying.

Jed closed his eyes again as Chaplain Stewart said, "This night I feel the wonderful presence of the Holy Spirit more than any other time we have gathered together. There is a oneness of mind between us and the Lord. If any of you have anything further you feel you wish to say, please do so."

One after another men petitioned their Lord in prayer.

As Jed wished he could also find the courage to speak – he had never prayed in public – he suddenly found himself saying, "I wants to thank ya, Father, fo' giving me a family to replace my own. Thank ya fo' Dog Jack and fo' Chaplain Stewart too."

Matt's voice was next. Gruff as if choked with emotion, he prayed, "Thank you, Lord, for friends and family – and for a good wife and a healthy and beautiful baby daughter."

Tom added, "Ah-men!" No one moved for some time. Each man remained in front of the campfire basking in its glow and the warmth that filled their souls. Finally, as if a signal had been given, one by one they turned and silently moved away from the fire.

Jed couldn't force himself to leave that place. As he sat staring into the dying embers, he continued to sense a peace such as he had never known before. He had listened as his chaplain friend described such an inner feeling or proclaimed its presence, but never before had he actually felt it inside himself. Reverend Stewart, who had also remained, drew near and put his arm around Jed.

"What is it, suh?" Jed asked. "I don' unnerstan' what I's feelin'."

"The Holy Spirit, Jed. He's been very present tonight. I think the Lord sent Him in His fullness to our gathering so He might prepare us for the emotional and physical battles before us."

"Don' wanna lose this feelin', suh. Always wanted ta be loved. Right now I feels like I loves ever'body an' God love me."

The chaplain nodded his head in agreement. "I know how you feel, Jed, but just because you move away from this fire doesn't mean you will lose it. All you ever have to do is pray often and keep thanking Him no matter what and you'll not lose your assurance that the Lord is right with you. You'd better get some rest now, son. We have a lot to do tomorrow."

Jed lifted Dog Jack up into his arms and started walking toward his bedroll.

"Night, Chaplain."

"Good night, Jed. God loves you. So do I."

Jed squeezed Dog Jack close to him. "Ya knows, boy, I don' think the chaplain's as crazy as I thought he must be, talkin' 'bout a 'Presence' so much. From the good feelin' I got in me tanight, I knows God mus' love me! ME, Jack! — the slave boy who don' even have a real las' name!"

Chapter 20
Christmas Presence

During the week before Christmas the usual war maneuvers changed drastically. At one point on their march along the Rappahannock River, they spied a small group of Confederate soldiers off to the side of the road.

"Ready! Aim! Fire!" came the order. As the men raised their rifles to shoot, a voice from their own regiment sent out a sudden cry of alarm to the enemy forces: "Down! Down, Johnny Rebs!"

Gray coats scattered through the brush. Their surprise attack had been ruined by one of their own men.

Jed, who'd been marching beside the chaplain, whispered, "Reverend Stewart, what's they gonna do ta that fella who yelled?" All eyes turned to look at the little private who'd issued the warning cry. When his sergeant walked over to him, the young man began to weep. Not much more than a boy, he wailed, "Sergeant, I'm sorry. I lost my best buddy yesterday. I just thought I couldn't stand to see nobody else's blood shed — not even the enemy's." His sobs turned into hysteria. "I can't stand it! I can't stand it!"

Jed realized this lad had become a victim of the war. His mind had snapped.

Chaplain Stewart went to the side of the youthful soldier, placed a consoling arm around him and began to talk. Jed could not hear the preacher's words, but knew the chaplain could console a hurting soldier better than anyone he'd ever known. Surely this man of God who so often had befriended him and had shown him such compassion had a special touch from the Lord.

Later on, Chaplain Stewart caught up to Jed and the others, explaining immediately to Jed, "We sent him to a hospital. No one could ever court-martial such a case. His nerves are in bad shape."

From that time on, both sides reacted differently than they had before. The fervor of hate changed to a feeling of compassion. It wasn't long until a Southern soldier hollered out to the 102nd as the Confederates waited in ambush, "Down, you fool Yanks! Down!"

Once their ambush position had been given away, the Rebel soldiers scattered. Still none of the Yanks fired, so Jed asked Matt, "Mistah Matt, how's come nobody's wantin' ta fight no mo'?"

"Too sick and tired of war, Jed. Nobody wants to see any more men lose their lives or their limbs."

"I was thinkin' maybe it was 'cause it's Christmas an' ever'body's homesick."

"That's certainly part of the answer," Chaplain Stewart interjected. "What a blessing! I'd be most pleased if they'd call a truce on the Lord's birthday." No one called a truce that Jed knew of, but no one waged war either.

On the night of December twenty-second, they were all huddled around the campfire to escape the winter chill. Their hearts were no warmer than their bodies, but Reverend Stewart coaxed them into singing a ditty one of the soldiers had dreamed up – "We drank from the same canteen" – but the light-hearted song didn't appear to improve the overall morale.

They stayed late beside the fire, chatting of home and family. Matt had just said, "Just imagine, this'll be my baby's first Christmas," when suddenly a noise came from the direction of the river which was not far away. Several of the men rushed down over the river bank, some promptly returning with packages in their arms. After taking the packages into their tents, they quickly reappeared carrying bottles which they took back to the river bank.

The whole episode aroused Jed's suspicions. Thinking Matt was the best one to question about such goings on, he asked, "What they doin'?"

"Trading supplies."

"With the enemy?"

"Why not? It's Christmas and they're out of supplies. We're out of snuff and tobacco. Have to have some pleasures in life. Last night a toy boat made from a board with a little sail attached came across the river with a note attached. 'U.S. Army. Gents. We need staples. You need tobacco. Let's trade tomorrow night.' That's what they're doing."

"But how'd them Jonny Rebs git ovah heah?" Jed whispered.

"In a row boat. How else?"

Jed's mouth dropped open, too speechless to reply. Later on in the evening he said to the chaplain, "Did ya know our men was exchangin' supplies wif' the enemy?"

Chaplain Stewart didn't answer for a moment, but then declared, "That's really not a shocker, Jed. Everyone's so tired of the horrors of this war. I just pray that the North can win soon, so the slaves will be free and we can all go home."

Jed looked down at the worn boots that housed his sore, bloody feet and nodded his head in agreement. "I 'spect that's the best thing the Lord could do fo' us."

Around midnight, Jed heard a stranger's voice talking with Matt. Peering out, he realized the man was clothed in a Confederate uniform. "What's a-goin' on?" he whispered to Dog Jack. "That's a Reb out thah!"

Seconds later the man in gray moved toward the river bank and Matt turned to go back to his tent.

"Mistah Matt," Jed whispered loud enough to be heard, "what's that fella doin' heah?"

Matt stopped just long enough to reply. "Just a soldier lonesome to see his brother who's in our company. Came over to talk for a while, but he has to get back before they find out he's missing. It's Christmas. Folks are extra lonely. Now go to sleep, Jed."

The next day as they continued on their march Jed looked around at the scattered remnant of the 102nd Regiment as they made their way into Frederick City, Maryland. He noticed the men's drawn, taut faces, their bodies bent from weariness and the low ebb of their morale.

Jed understood that the time of year had much to do with the troops' sagging spirits. The date was December twenty-third. Behind the mask-like faces, the men continued to brood about home, kinfolk and Christmas.

Not so for Jed. Since he had lost his own family Matt, Chaplain Stewart and Dog Jack were all he cared much about. Although they weren't blood relatives, they had become like kinfolks to him. Those three were all he had.

As they shuffled along, Matt turned to him and asked, "How're your feet, boy?"

"They's all right, Mistah Matt," Jed lied. How desperately he wished Matt hadn't mentioned such a sore subject. The pain was only tolerable as long as he forced himself to think about other things.

Weeks before, the tattered remnants he called socks had given out and there were no more to be had, the clothing supplies having been long exhausted. With no socks to protect his feet from the friction of the leather, great blisters had raised, broken open and oozed pus, then bled.

Chaplain Stewart had taken him to the sutler — the peddler who pitched a tent where they camped and followed them wherever they went. During most of the war the sutler had somehow managed to keep cans of fruit and milk on hand along with stationery, pens, tobacco and even some clothing, but his supplies were running out. Looking at the peddler's wares, Chaplain Stewart had asked, "No socks available, sir?"

"Not for a long time, Chaplain. Sorry."

Next the chaplain sought the help of a nurse who gave Jed a roll of bandage. Every night Jed had carefully washed and wrapped his feet. That had helped some.

But each morning when he tried to don his shoes, the pain was so excruciating that he wondered whether it would be best to go barefoot or just to sleep with his shoes on.

This particular December morning he found that circumstances were making that decision for him. Trudging wearily forward along the river bank, he watched the cold, swirling waters of the Rappahannock and yearned to dip his bruised feet. As he daydreamed about the soothing effects of such an encounter, the sole of his right shoe collided with a rock and thrust him forward. The tired and worn threads on the bottom of his shoe gave way and the sole flipped backward. Jed's sore, swollen toes protested the impact so acutely that he fell to the ground in agonizing pain.

"Jed!" Chaplain Stewart cried. Immediately he was kneeling beside him.

"I's all right, suh," Jed claimed as he sat up and began to examine his shoe, wondering what to do with the loose sole.

"You can't walk with that thing flapping," the chaplain protested and ripped the cord off his canteen. Leaning down, he pulled the sole up tight to Jed's shoe, then deftly tied the cord into a tight knot.

"There," he sighed, "that won't last long, but at least it should stay for the rest of the day. A rumor just came down the line that the Colonel intends to stop the march early today." Extending a hand to Jed, he helped him stand.

Matt, who had fallen back, was marking time for them to catch up. As the two approached him, a frown of concern crossed his brow. "You gonna make it, Jed, boy?" he asked.

Jed nodded affirmatively and the three of them fell in step together. A whimper from behind them suddenly brought Jack to Jed's mind. He whirled around and saw that Jack was limping, blood seeping from the bottom of his right paw.

Jed tried to grin. "Well, well! Ya tryin' ta be my twin?" He bent down and reached out. The dog gratefully fell into his arms. Jed lifted his friend to his shoulder and Jack's head relaxed against the curve in his neck. As Jed continued to methodically march forward, Dog Jack's bones seemed to grind through his flesh and deep into his arms.

The ache was like the tightening of the jaws on a steel vice. Small pebbles made their way into the toe of his shoe and ground into Jed's flesh.

Matt noticed the grimace on Jed's face and walked closer to him, protesting, "Jed, put that fool dog down! He's too heavy to carry! – Come to think of it, he's not the fool! You are!"

Jed thought his weary canine friend must have fallen off to sleep, for he seemed to get heavier by the minute. His silver collar pressed, then cut into Jed's skin. Yet somehow he couldn't part with the comforting warmth of Jack's body. If only Matt knew how much he wished he could put his burden down, but Jack's close presence was the one thing that gave him a sense of well-being. No matter how much he wanted to reach down and pull the stones from his shoe, no matter how desperately he wished he could rub his arms to get the blood circulating again – to rid himself of the prickly needles that jabbed his arm – he simply could not.

When Jed made no move to put the dog down, Matt persisted, "If you think that mutt needs to be carried, then give him here!"

For the first time Jed noticed Matt's hollow cheeks. His usually robust friend's eyes were shadowed by dark circles. Matt had not only lost weight, but also his pink-cheeked, healthy glow.

"Sorry, Mistah Matt, today he's my dog. Besides, you looks like ya cain't drag yo'self anothah step," Jed argued.

Matt breathed heavily, then answered in a tone of disgust, "You shouldn't talk, boy. Keep carrying that dog and you're never going to make it."

"Ho!" the sergeant called out. The regiment came to a halt. "We're going to make camp in that field. Everybody fall out."

"Before they fall down!" Matt grumbled.

Jed stumbled into the field. With one hand and much difficulty he removed his knapsack, then carefully placed the dog on top of it. Jack never stirred.

Glancing around at the other soldiers busy setting up

camp, Jed had no strength left to help. He plunked himself down on the ground beside Jack and lovingly flopped his aching arm around his friend. Content, he soon joined Jack in sleep.

When Jed finally awakened, night had set in. Stars winked back from the sky above him. He heard music. Seeing a glow in the sky, his eyes followed it down to the horizon and discovered that some of the men had built a campfire and were singing Christmas carols.

As the words "Noel, Noel" drifted to him, he found himself fighting back a nostalgic tear determined to find its way down his cheek. He wondered how he could be homesick – there was nothing left for him to be homesick for. He could never talk to his mother or any other family member again. Shivering from the winter cold, he once again reached for Jack to console him, but was startled to find that Jack wasn't there.

As quickly as his aching bones would permit, Jed raised himself to a sitting position to look for his dog. He was grateful to find that Chaplain Stewart was standing nearby looking down at him. As always, the chaplain was there when he needed him.

"I put that blanket over you, son," Reverend Stewart said. "I was going to take your shoes off to rest your feet, but I thought that could wait. Sleep seemed to be the thing you needed most."

Jed stretched. "Ya seen Jack, suh?"

The chaplain smiled. "Don't worry about him, Jed. He fends for himself very well. He'll be back soon. In the meantime I've got some water boiling to wash your feet. You stay here while I get it."

Jed watched the chaplain walk over to the log fire. He had never known a more considerate man – the one and only person Jed ever met who lived the faith he professed to believe in.

When Reverend Stewart returned, he placed the water beside Jed, then leaned down and tenderly began to extract Jed's aching feet from his shoes.

"Grit your teeth, Jed. You have dried blood in there. It's going to hurt something fierce when that gives way."

Bracing the ground behind him with both hands, Jed grimaced as the chaplain gave one quick tug on this right shoe, but then the foot was free. A cold breeze brushed across the open sores with a vengeance.

Reverend Stewart removed a white handkerchief from his pocket and dipped it in the boiling water. Squeezing the excess water from it, he dabbed gently at Jed's swollen foot.

Jed sat upright. "You ain't gonna be a-washin' my feet! No, suh! You don' need ta wash no black boy's feet!"

Reverend Stewart pulled back for a moment, his face stunned.

"Jed!" he protested. "How can you say such a thing? The Lord washed men's feet." The chaplain continued to clean and bandage Jed's right foot, then added, "If it didn't humble Him too much, it certainly won't bother me."

Jed searched the chaplain's eyes. He had seen many things expressed through them, but never anything contemptible or mean – only kindness, love and compassion.

When the task of bandaging the foot was finished, Chaplain Stewart seated himself on the ground beside Jed and put an arm around his shoulder. "Jed, wait here," he directed. "The circuit rider managed to catch up with us and delivered the mail while you were sleeping. He had Christmas packages for everyone and I've got yours over by my belongings. I'll go get it."

Jed couldn't help but wonder what the chaplain was talking about. He had no one anywhere who would send him mail at Christmas – or at any other time for that matter.

Reverend Stewart returned and handed him a large box. Jed tore at the strings and gasped as the contents became visible – a beautiful pair of brown leather boots and two pairs of handknit white socks.

"These cain't be mine, suh!" he declared. "They's yours, ain't they? I cain't take 'em."

The chaplain shook his head emphatically from side to

side. "No, Jed, they belong to you. Look at the address." Jed lifted the brown wrapping paper up to peer at it in the dim glow from the campfire. The printed words, JED SUH, stood out plainly. He looked up at the chaplain in wonderment.

"Who, suh? Who'd know?" he queried.

"The Lord doth provide."

Jed stared at the paper once more. "S-T-E-W-A-R-T," he read aloud from the return address in the corner. "Ya had yo' folks send 'em – to ME? Why, suh? Why did ya?" Jed could not comprehend the preacher's reasoning.

"Because I wanted to get you something special on Christ's birthday – because you're special to me. Almost like a son."

In the soft yellow glow from the fire, Jed was certain he saw tears glistening on the chaplain's cheeks. Motionless and quiet, the two friends sat together, staring at the crackling campfire and listening to the words, "SILENT NIGHT, HOLY NIGHT..." as singing filled the air. Jed turned to Reverend Stewart, the increasingly familiar lump in his throat growing larger.

"Ya mean that, suh?" Jed whispered. "Ya mean what ya jes' said?"

"With all my heart." The hate, frustration and pain of Jed's inner turmoil surfaced at that moment. All his pent-up emotions gave way. With a great sob he threw himself into Chaplain Stewart's arms and cried, "Oh, Chaplain! I's so glad the Lord sent ya ta me!"

Reverend Stewart pulled Jed toward him and held him close. "So am I, son," he confided, his own voice cracking with emotion. "So am I."

While the men sat on logs encircling the campfire, Tom Drysdale lifted his harmonica to his lips. During his rendition of the tune "Tenting Tonight" the men joined in, singing the lyrics. The words "wishing for the war to cease" had never been more meaningful to the bedraggled, homesick men of the 102nd Pennsylvania Regiment.

Then abruptly Tom changed his theme to Christmas music. The men joined in with enthusiasm to sing "Joy to the World" as Tom played. Jed watched their mood change during the more sentimental pieces. By the time they'd finished singing "Silent Night," Chaplain Stewart was singing above the other voices. One by one the men dropped out of the chorus, staring into the fire as if they were mesmerized. Most were dewy eyed, some couldn't prevent tears from slipping down their cheeks. Jed knew they were thinking of home and recalling the joy-filled holidays of their past.

He understood their feelings of homesickness, even though his were not the same. Both the aroma of the burning wood and the brilliant flames held consolation for him. The blazing camp fire's warmth had taken the chill from his own body on that cold December night and replaced it with a sense of contentment.

The harmonica music and the singing had ceased. At a moment when everything was quiet except for the crackling of the burning wood, Reverend Stewart rose before the men. "My heart is heavy tonight, brave soldiers. During this war I have seen so many men go down in the heat of battle – strangers slipping into eternity. I have no recourse but to pray fervently for their souls, for many on the battlefield I do not know."

Chaplain Stewart's voice deepened with emotion as he continued. "But you men – you are like my family. We've shared feast and famine, joy and sorrow. We've become such close friends. I pray constantly for each of you because God has put me in a position of shepherding you – and often I feel I am failing you miserably.

"The Lord is my Shepherd, but I cannot speak with that same certainty for any of you. Some of you valiant souls came into this bloody war as nothing more than boys, but within days the reality of war made combat men out of you. My concern is not for your abilities as soldiers or your faithfulness to the cause of freedom, but it grieves me greatly that I cannot truthfully say what state each of your souls are in.

"Because I feel at this significant emotion-filled moment

God is looking down on us with compassion to prepare us for the battles which are to come, I feel the urgent need to ask you to let the Lord come into your hearts. It says in the Good Book that 'no man can come to the Father except by me.' My dear beloved friends, before this night is over, I want you to be able to rest assured that you would go to heaven if you were killed in battle. There is no way for you to do that except to repent and ask God's Son, Jesus, to come into your heart. Will you bow your heads and, knowing that God is a loving and forgiving Heavenly Father, ask Him to forgive and cleanse you of all your sins and accept you as a part of His Kingdom?

"I'm not telling you what you should pray, I am simply telling you how. Please take this opportunity to bow your heads and in the privacy of your hearts sincerely ask His forgiveness. I don't want to have to fret one more time about the state of one of your souls."

It seemed to Jed that even the fire was hushed during the time the men prayed. In Jed's own mind, he cried out to the Lord and asked Him to forgive his bitterness toward Master Cooper, to the white race in general, to the South for demeaning his race and even to the Union men who'd killed his family. His heart cried, "Oh, LORD, fo'gives me fo' all them bad feelin's I's been hidin' in my heart. I's nothin' but a sinner an' I's sorry." A warmth penetrated him — body, mind and spirit — one he knew was not from the fire. As he raised his head he sensed the reality of God's presence and knew that the Lord had answered his prayer.

Chapter 21
An Answer

For a long time Jed sat huddled close to the man who had called him "son," in deep thought and basking in the warm feeling which lingered. Finally, he leaned forward and announced decisively, "Think I's gonna go lookin' for Dog Jack. Not like him ta be gone fo' so long."

"Then I'll go with you."

As they arose to leave the site of the campfire, Matt looked at them with raised eyebrows and asked, "Where're you two going?"

"Jack's gone," Jed informed him. "We's gonna hunt 'im."

Without another word Matt rose to join them.

"Jack, Jack! Here, Dog Jack!" they called frantically as they walked into the dark still night. There was no response. After a half hour of calling and searching the chaplain suggested, "We can cover the territory better if we go in different directions. Matt, why don't you go to the left? I'll circle to the right. Jed, you walk straight ahead."

Wordlessly, each searcher set out toward the area assigned to him. As Jed inched his way over the rugged terrain, he stopped at every piece of soft ground, every crackling noise. A twig snapped in front of him and Jed's heart raced faster than it had the time Matt had taken him to the harness races, but then he realized it was only a startled rabbit darting about. How he'd have welcomed the sound of a familiar bark.

Suddenly tiredness consumed him. He paused on a hillside, struggling to master the courage and strength to go on. The winter wind whipped about him chilling his body and his heart. Thoughts of his missing dog forced him to move forward, his raw feet fighting the confinement of his stiff new boots. Every bone, every muscle in his body joined in protest as the night wore on.

Fear gripped his heart as he met Matt and the chaplain for the third time. Golden rays from the sun indicated the dawn of a new day and Jed could see in the dim early morning light Reverend Stewart's and Matt's sagging shoulders and discouraged expressions. Their search had also been futile.

"Let's go back to camp and begin again at daybreak," the chaplain suggested, but Jed shook his head in disapproval.

"You both kin go back, suh, but I's gonna stay 'til I finds 'im — even if it takes me fo'ever."

"Jed, we're all too tired to hunt anymore," Matt argued impatiently. "If we're going to be able to find him at all, it'll be in the morning when we can see better."

By then Jed's thoughts were jumbled, his head burning hot, his legs and arms aching from weakness. Every part of his body was bursting with pain. His throbbing chest felt as though a great pressure was pushing against his lungs from all sides. He could scarcely take a breath.

"Ya think somebody'd hurt him fo' his collah? Or — he din't seem too perky whiles we was marchin' — don' think he was sick, do ya? ...HAS ta find 'im!" he mumbled. Staggering forward, he fell face down on the cold ground, unconscious.

Matt scooped him up in his arms. "You crazy boy, you're burning with fever!" he exclaimed with alarm. "Here, chaplain, feel his head."

Chaplain Stewart placed the palm of his hand against Jed's forehead. "He must have far more wrong with him than sore feet, Matt. We'd better get him to the hospital tent."

Hearing the chaplain's evaluation of Jed's condition,

Matt gently worked his arms under Jed's and, carrying his limp friend, began making his way down the hill. Reverend Stewart walked beside him, holding Jed's feet.

A bearded doctor making his rounds and checking on patients glanced up as Matt and the chaplain carried Jed into the hospital tent.

"War casualty?" he asked them.

"Manner of speaking," Chaplain Stewart answered.

While Matt and the chaplain stood anxiously by, the doctor examined the patient. His expression was grave as finally he looked back at them.

"Looks serious," he stated flatly. "It's quite possible that he has pneumonia in both lungs."

Matt was bewildered. "You'd never have known it," he commented. "He never complained about anything – not even his sore feet!"

"Sore feet?" the doctor inquired. After carefully removing the unconscious lad's boots and socks, he unwound the soiled bandages. Blisters and open sores oozing blood and pus caused the doctor to step back and stare.

"You mean this boy has been WALKING?" the physician asked. "These feet are so infected that I don't know how he could even STAND on them!"

Chaplain Stewart stared at the sores which were worse than any he had ever seen. "It's incredible!" he exclaimed. "They didn't look that bad in the light of the fire. And he's been walking for miles hunting his dog!"

Once again the doctor stared down at the unconscious soldier on the cot, then up at his two friends. "If a dog means that much to him, you'd better try to find it. This lad's going to have a tough time making it. We'll do everything we can, but it'll help if he has something to live for." The doctor put his hand to his beard and stroked his long whiskers as if deep in thought. "Even then," he spoke in solemn tones, "he has very little chance."

Speechless, Matt and the chaplain stared at one another, trying to decide what they should do. Finally Reverend Stewart spoke. "I don't think the dog's even alive, sir.

We've hunted half the night for him."

With a shrug of his shoulders, the doctor dismissed them. "I sure hope you find him. Now, if you don't mind a bit of professional advice, I suggest you two go to bed for a while before you both wind up in the same condition as your friend here."

Both Matt and the chaplain returned to their blankets and tried to follow the doctor's suggestion, but each spent a restless few hours. Neither seemed surprised to find the other meeting daybreak with a new determination to find Jed's dog.

"Matt," Reverend Stewart explained, "I'm going to find the colonel and see if I can get permission to take some of the men with us to help hunt for Jack."

"Go ahead, sir," Matt concurred. "I'm going to go check on Jed."

When Chaplain Stewart approached the colonel's tent, he saw no signs of movement, so was certain he must still be asleep. The officer was known to have the disposition of a frustrated grizzly bear when awakened in the morning.

Gathering courage, the chaplain cleared his throat and announced in a loud voice, "Colonel, sir? Chaplain Stewart here."

"What is it you want?" a snarling voice replied.

"I've an urgent need, sir, and I want your permission to recruit some volunteers to help."

"For what purpose, chaplain?" the stern voice asked.

"To find the company mascot, sir."

The flap on the tent flew up and the colonel's face appeared. All Reverend Stewart could think of was an old English bulldog.

"Are you telling me that you woke me to ask for help to go find a...DOG?" he growled. "Chaplain, I have thousands of MEN to worry about!"

The tent flap jerked shut and Reverend Stewart stood in silence and dismay. At last he gathered enough courage to approach the commanding office again. "But, Colonel," Reverend Stewart pleaded, "the doctor says the dog might save a boy's life!"

The chaplain continued to stand, staring at the closed tent flap, wondering if the colonel had become so calloused by the war that he no longer cared about saving precious lives. The flap on the tent flew open and once more the colonel's face appeared. But this time, to the chaplain's relief, he sensed he had touched a soft spot in the officer's professional armor.

"Why didn't you say so, Chaplain?" he demanded. "You must realize I am an exhausted, war-weary soldier. Take the men you need, but be back by noon – we've a war to fight!"

With a smile of relief on his face, Chaplain Stewart snapped to attention, gave a salute and a "YES, SIR!" Then he turned to leave.

"Reverend Stewart?" the colonel called after him. The chaplain spun about.

"Yes, sir?"

"Good luck, sir. And God go with you."

"Thank you, sir," the chaplain answered gratefully as he hurried on his way.

Matt approached him, along with four other men from Company F. From the looks on their faces, Reverend Stewart knew Matt had filled them in on the need for a search party.

"How's Jed?" the chaplain asked Matt.

"Out of his head, sir. The doctor just shakes his head when he looks at him."

"Come on, then. The colonel said we could all help if we're back by noon. If each of us takes a radius of about five hundred feet and works his way back here, we can cover the area faster."

During the next few hours, cries came from all directions: "Here, Jack! Jack, here, fellow!" But the calls were of no avail. As they met on the hillside at eleven thirty the chaplain declared, "It looks hopeless to me. You know Jack would come or at least cry out if he could hear us."

An unhappy and disheveled Matt agreed. "That's true,

sir, but maybe he's unconscious."

"Or dead," Reverend Stewart added. "Jed always worried that someone would kill him to get his collar."

The flush on Matt's face grew flame red. Infuriated, he cried, "They'd better not!" Shaking his fist in the air he added, "I'll break their fool necks if I ever find out someone did that!"

Turning to the others the chaplain said, "I promised the colonel I'd have you back by noon, so we'll have to abandon the search now." "Abandon the search." His own words echoed in his ears. The tug in his heart told him they were not only abandoning the search but also the boy and his dog. In silence they climbed the hill together, each engrossed in his own special memories of Jed and Dog Jack. The chaplain could find no words to comfort them or himself.

Nearing the hospital tent, Reverend Stewart said to Matt, "I think I need to admit something to you. If there is such a lowly culprit, I would probably want to wring his neck even more than you! That's a terrible admission for a man of the cloth to have to make."

Matt patted the chaplain on his shoulder and consoled him, "No, it's not, sir. I think more of you for having said it."

Once inside the tent they found the bearded doctor leaning down close to Jed. "How is he, sir?" Reverend Stewart whispered.

"Still out of his head. Keeps mumbling about Jack – is that the dog?"

The chaplain frowned. "Yes, sir, I'm afraid it is."

Heaving a great sigh, the doctor acknowledged, "That means you didn't find him. Frankly, he's so far gone now, I don't think even the dog's presence would help."

Chaplain Stewart looked down at the dark-skinned boy he had come to love. "But he might have helped," he admitted. "I think Jed believes the dog was the only thing that ever needed him. But he was wrong. Oh, was he wrong!"

Even Reverend Stewart was surprised at the extent of

the emotion he felt. He swallowed in an attempt to gain his composure, then added softly, "I need him, too."

Matt, standing beside him, confessed, "I guess I didn't realize how much he means to me either, Chaplain."

After a moment of silent prayer, Reverend Stewart raised his head and confronted Matt with renewed hopefulness in his voice. "Just now when I was praying I'm certain the Lord was giving me an idea. You stay here with Jed. I'll be gone the rest of the day. I hope I can bring a Christmas present back to him – and to us!"

"Where're you going, sir?" Matt asked.

"To find what I believe Jed needs. Matt, if you've never prayed before, start now. From the looks of our boy – it'll take a miracle to save him."

Seeing Matt linger by Jed's side, the doctor finally said, "If you're going to stay here, you might as well be of some use. Here, keep sponging off his forehead with cool water."

"Yes, sir."

The hands on his pocket watch seemed to stand still for Matt as he kept his vigil at Jed's bedside. Occasionally Jed cried out and thrashed. Matt faithfully wiped the cool damp cloth soothingly across his forehead.

Through his parched lips the boy cried, "Jack! Jack!" again and again. Matt wanted to take the delirious young man into his arms and comfort him. How he wished he could do more to help! The only other thing he knew to do was to pray – and he didn't do that very well, for it was something he seldom took time to do.

The doctor came by at regular intervals to check on Jed's condition. Each time Matt carefully scanned his face for a sign of encouragement, but found none.

After several of the doctor's silent rounds, Matt could stand no more. "Doctor," he said in a soft voice, so as not to disturb Jed, "is he going to make it?" The doctor made no reply, but shook his head hopelessly as if he could see no way for Jed to get better.

Unaccustomed as he was at petitioning the Lord for favors, Matt knelt beside the bed. Tears flowed down his cheeks as he whispered, "Please, Lord, PLEASE save Jed's life. I know I don't talk with you often, but I always know you are there. Please," he pleaded, "I'm not asking for me, I'm asking for Jed."

Outside the hospital tent the chaplain's horse whinnied. Moments later he strode in the door carrying a small pup. Upon checking the young dog, Matt exclaimed, "That's a miniature Dog Jack – even has that same goofy spot around his eyes!"

Chaplain Stewart's eyes twinkled. "He's Dog Jack's son, Matt. I'd heard that Pollyanna'd had a litter, so I went over to her regiment to see. Sure enough, this little fellow couldn't look more like our mascot if he tried."

At that moment the doctor returned. "Is that his dog?"

"No, sir," Matt answered, "but he's a miniature version." They all stood around Jed's bed as Chaplain Stewart placed the pup in the curve of the former slave boy's neck. Silently and anxiously they waited. "Lord, we'll take a miracle, please," the chaplain prayed.As they watched the pup stretched his nose toward Jed's face and lapped his cheek with it's tiny pink tongue. The three men held their breath, hoping and praying silently for some reaction from their ailing friend and patient. Any movement would be an improvement.

Then, every so slightly, Jed stirred. Slowly he opened one eye and looked down, as if trying to focus his eyes to be certain he was seeing accurately. Upon viewing the miniature of Dog Jack, he tried to force a smile. "Welcome home, Little Jack," he whispered weakly. "Welcome home."

LIVING HISTORY GALLERY...

Photos taken at Gettysburg's 125th Anniversary

July 2-4, 1988

Sentry on duty.

Men discuss the times.

Rifles ready — men waiting.

Soldier sips from his canteen.

Enemy is sighted.

Cannons loaded — cannons roar. . . .

Ready, aim — fire!

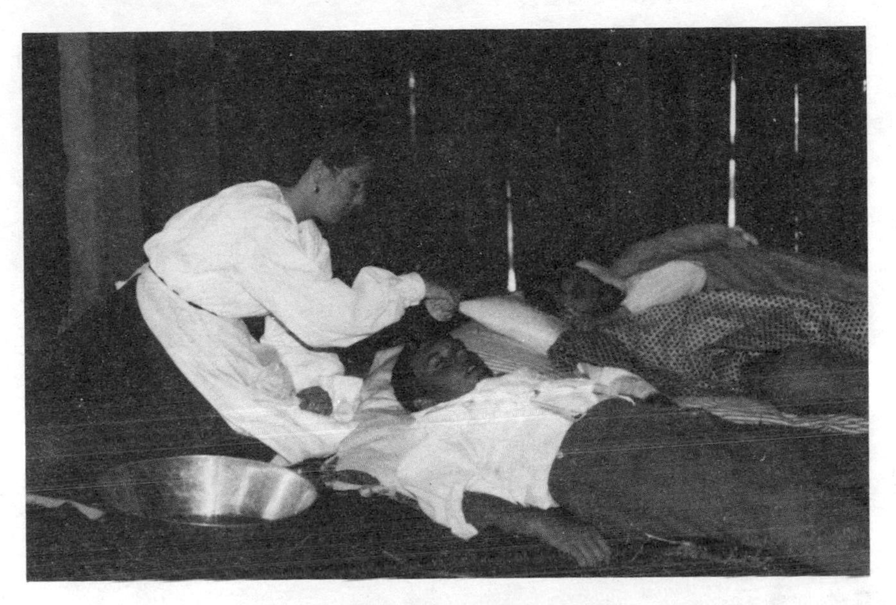

Ministering to wounded.

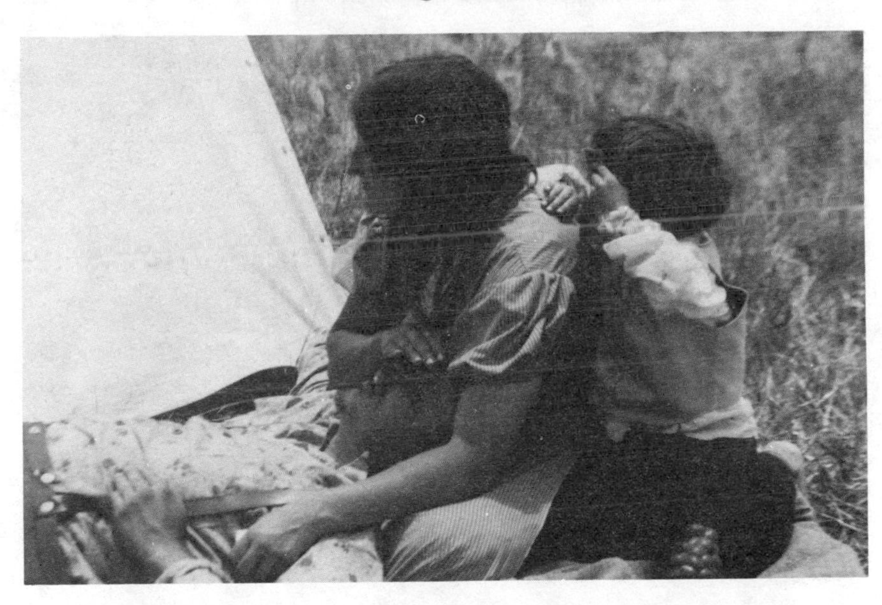

Confederates help wounded — clothes need mending too!

Sutler examines wares; confederate chats with girl.

Pondering next maneuver.

Dressed for the ball.

Corresponding with home — moments to relax.

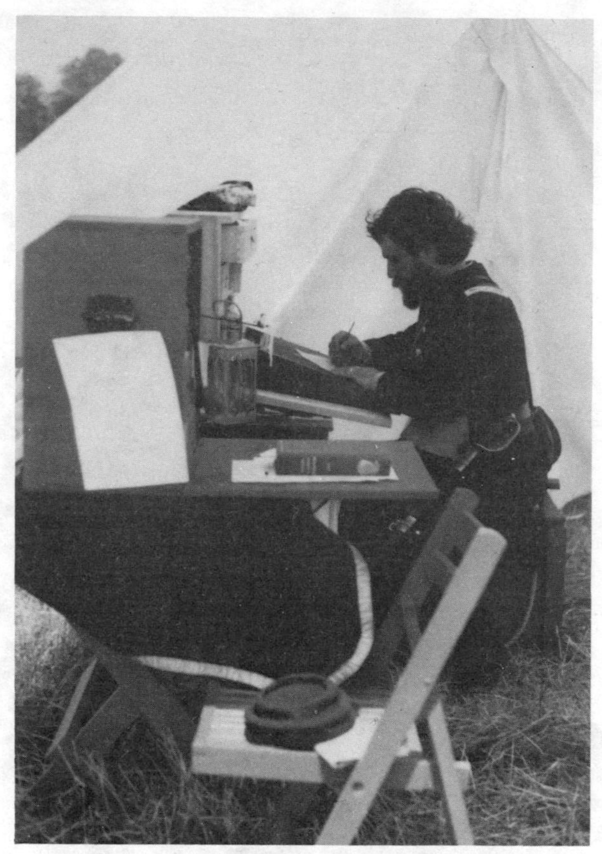

Thoughts of home, sweet home. . . .

We gratefully acknowledge the following reenactors who so willingly posed for the Living History Gallery:

Dr. Drew Allbritten
Chris Aleo
Richard Baldino
John Balko
Keith Baylor
Fr. Winthrop Brainerd
Charlene Bullard
Frances Burroughs
Patty Elmer-Bush
Renee Elizabeth Allbritten
Kelly Centorani
William Schuster
Michael E. Crimens
John Culp
William Kenny
Michael Knaff
Richard Leisenring
Roberta Lukas
Michael J. Lipsky
Major James A. Major
Robert Milligan
Paul C. Miller
David G. Morris
Brian O'Connor
Joseph Pereira
Ernest W. Peterkin
William, Cheryl Peterson and child
Charles Smeltzer
Arthur Stacey
Steve Topper
Dr. Thomas Adrian Wheat
Robert A. Wilburn, Jr.

BIBLIOGRAPHY

Camp, March and Battlefield, Alexander M. Stewart, 1864.

Billy Yank and Johnny Reb, Miers, Earl Schenck – Rand McNally, 1959.

Gettysburg: The Final Fury, Bruce Catton – Doubleday, 1974.